CHARITY SHIELDS AND THE BUILDING PLOT

JOHN GUTHRIE

CHAPTER ONE

C harity said, "Eric? But that's a boy's name."

"Yes," Angie replied. "It seemed a good idea when we saw that he was a boy. I told you we'd had a boy."

"But that was years ago, and it was just the sort of thing that married couples do. Like going to the Canaries, and extending the patio. It wasn't something to keep in the mind. When you said would I have 'the little monster' for three weeks, I thought you meant the cat." She widened her eyes. "A *boy*."

"Oh, he's not so bad."

"Not so bad as what?"

"Well, he *is* high-spirited, lively, inquisitive. A typical boy."

"That means horrible. I had a brother, who had friends."

"No, no. Oh, no. Not *horrible*. He's still only eleven."

"When you say 'inquisitive', do you mean peeping into bathrooms and bedrooms when I'm naked, that sort of thing?"

"No, no. But if he does anything like that, just shoo him away and tell him not to be silly."

"You mean walk over to him, put my hand on his shoulder and lead him out."

"Well, it's up to you how you do it. I mean, it's not such a big thing these days."

Charity decided to give up on that one. The bathroom door had a lock, and she had one of those rubber wedges that she could use for the bedroom door.

"When you say 'lively', does that involve a lot of noise."

"Well, he can be a bit loud at times."

"He won't have an electric guitar, will he?"

"He won't *have* one."

"You're talking in italics again. What does that mean?"

"He makes electric guitar sounds. With his mouth. As children do."

"So, '*wow, wow, wow*'.

"Yes, that sort of thing."

"You know, Angie, I can't help feeling that there are other people who are better suited to looking after Eric for three weeks. Better qualified, you might say."

"Well, you see …"

"No-one else would have him."

"No, not *that*. It just came at a very bad time for a lot of people."

"I can imagine. And after you failed to persuade a lot of people, you turned to me. I'm the last resort, aren't I?"

"Oh, I wouldn't say that."

"Only because it's true. Anyway, I'm not surprised that I'm the last resort. I know all about me. I *live* with me. I have to put up with me. I wouldn't even trust me with the cat. You must be desperate to ask me."

Angie turned on the irresistibly sad look. "Yes, Charity. I'm, we're, desperate. And we've turned to you for help."

"Okay. But no complaints. I want a waiver. No liability. If he goes on a raft in the canal, and it sinks …"

"There isn't a canal round here."

"River, then! We have a river. Or if he runs in front of a bus. Or swallows arsenic."

"Do you *have* arsenic?"

"Bleach, then."

"He's not a toddler. He knows not to drink bleach."

"Okay. Leave the bleach. There are hundreds of ways in which lively and inquisitive boys, your words, can be badly injured or killed. If that happens, I don't want everyone blaming me."

"No-one will blame you."

Charity sighed. "Well, as the last resort, and because in spite of your low opinion of me, you were my best friend, and even though you haven't visited me for years, or done much to keep in touch…I agree to do this big thing. As soon as you've left, I'd better stock up with the ghastly stuff that boys eat. What does he like?"

"He's very fond of baked beans. He eats a lot of baked beans."

"A boy who eats a lot of baked beans."

It was almost enough to make her change her mind.

Stoically, she pressed on. "What else?"

"Oh, the usual things. Fish fingers. Sausages. Chips. Waffles. The usual breakfast cereals. Fruit pies. Fruit yoghurts."

"Fruit yoghurts? Why, that's nearly healthy. Just the sugar overload."

"We've tried healthier options. It's very difficult with children and food."

"Yes, I remember my brother and his table tantrums. It's mostly a boy thing. An early stage in proving their manhood. Look, I'm killing myself. How manly can you be?"

"And as your parents probably found, in the end you think 'sod it', I can't take any more. If he wants junk food, let him have junk food."

"I hope no-one sees me buying this stuff. I'll sneak through the self-service area. I don't want someone standing behind me in a queue, thinking what a terrible mother I am, or worse, thinking it's for myself."

"I didn't know you bothered about what people thought. You never used to. Or is this an image thing? Fish fingers and waffles don't go with being an eccentric, solitary spinster who grows her own herbs and eats things that grow in the hedgerows?"

"Do you want me to have your monster or not?"

"Yes. Please."

"Then, stop the insults. Especially when they're true."

"Thanks so much, Charity. We're very grateful."

"Glad to help."

"Thursday morning? About eight? We have to catch the plane at seven pm."

"Why aren't you taking him with you?"

"We ... need a little time to ourselves. You know how it ... well, no, you don't."

"Oh, I do. That's why I live alone and stop all that before it starts. I won't make the same mistake once."

"Well, having some company will be a nice change for you. Like a little holiday."

"Oh. For me, his presence is the ingredient for a little holiday; for you, his absence is the ingredient for a big holiday."

"I wouldn't say that exactly. You make us sound like horrible parents."

"Not at all. I'm sure that after three weeks of Eric, I shall be seen as a horrible temporary aunty."

Angie said, "Oh, it won't be that bad."

"In my experience," Charity said, "things are always either that bad or worse."

CHAPTER TWO

Eric didn't *look* like the villainous type, but Charity knew better than to trust appearances. She thought that Angie should have stayed to provide a short training session, perhaps left her with an instruction manual. But after an unimpressive attempt to display sorrow at parting from their son, she and Terry almost flew down the drive, and drove away as though they were being pursued.

"My Dad likes to drive quickly," said Eric.

"Oh, he always drives like that, does he?" She added quietly, "Not just when he's leaving his son."

"He wants to have an XJ6."

"Does he? Are we still talking about cars?"

"*Yes.* I just said he wants an XJ6."

"Shall I tell you something shocking, Eric? I don't know what an XJ6 is."

"He told Mum that it's like driving a naked woman."

Charity pushed aside pertinent questions and comments on the grounds that it would make things worse, and would require her to make acerbic comments about Eric's father.

"Have you had breakfast, Eric?"

"No. There wasn't time."

Such a hurry. "Your mother said that you like Sugar Flakes. I popped to the local shop for some."

"I prefer Choco-Wheats."

"Ah. I wasn't told that one. Do you think you could manage some Sugar Flakes?"

"Yeah. Why not?"

"Why not indeed?"

While Eric forced down some Sugar Flakes, Charity made a few rounds of toast, and put them ready on the table with margarine and two types of marmalade.

Rewarding herself with a mug of coffee, she sat down at a respectable distance from the visitor.

"This is the wrong marmalade."

"Well, have the other one."

"Does that one have shreds, too?"

"Oh," she said with fake exasperation. "She didn't say, and I didn't think. I forgot that there are children who can't chew marmalade shreds and who must have it in the form of shredless jelly. Is that why some people call it jelly? Oh, well. Try to dig the jelly part out, leaving the shreds behind. It'll make it more interesting."

"More of a pain."

"It depends on how you look at it. It can be a pain, or it can make it more interesting. It's what you want it to be."

"It's a pain."

"So are you, my little prince. But only if I let you. It's up to me to find the good in you and improve you."

"I don't need improving."

"You're perfect, are you?"

"I didn't say that."

"Well, if you don't need improving, how can you not be perfect?"

"You're just twisting things round. I'm not perfect, but I don't need improving. Especially by you."

"Why am I not suited to the task?"

"You don't even have a husband."

"That's because I don't want a husband."

"That's what old women who can't find a husband say."

"You think I'm old?"

"Well, you will be."

"So will you. Provided that you survive three weeks with me."

"What are you going to do? Murder me?"

Charity leaned forward and looked deeply into his eyes. "I might do, Eric. I'm very interested in crimes. I find them often fascinating. I study the methods and the newspaper accounts, going such a long way back. There's an assumption that criminals are always caught eventually. Not so. The brutal, impetuous, emotional, careless ones are caught, often very easily. But the ones who plan carefully, anticipating potential errors, and avoiding them are the ones who aren't caught. I try to think as they do. I plan murders, Eric. I work out how I'm going to kill someone, without leaving any evidence, any clues. I plan robberies by the same method."

Eric was becoming worried. Very nervously, he said, "Why? Are you going to do any of those things?"

She sat back and smiled, with just enough of a naughty glint to keep him alert.

"No, Eric. It's what I consider to be the essential background to my little hobby."

"What hobby's that?"

"Do you promise not to tell anyone?"

"Yes."

"Not Mum and Dad, not any other family, not friends, not even the police?"

His eyes were wide. He tried to say, 'Yes', then thought that perhaps the correct answer was, 'No'. The result was a shrill squeak. He coughed and swallowed and settled for, "No. I won't tell anyone."

"I'd be very annoyed if you did. *Very* annoyed."

"I won't tell anyone. I promise."

"The investigation of crimes, Eric. That's my hobby."

CHAPTER THREE

At least she distracted Eric from his sufferings with the marmalade. Although she immediately had to disappoint him by telling him that she wasn't a private investigator, and just tried to work out the identity of criminals, theoretically, from newspaper and internet reports.

"How successful are you?"

"I'm not. Not entirely my fault. Newspaper cases tend to fizzle out. It's always been that way. People don't have long attention spans, and newspapers always want to move on to the next exciting thing. A front page story about a murder is shoved inside because a politician has said something controversial or a famous person in an unreality show has eaten an earwig. After a few days, everyone seems to lose interest, including the police. So, I don't know whether or not what I've done before that was on the right lines."

"Why don't you go and ask the police?"

"Because this isn't a story. The police would say that it's confidential, I'm not authorised, and, with suspiciously narrowed eyes, what is my interest in the matter?"

"Tell them you're an amateur detective."

"Again, this isn't a story. Forget Sherlock Holmes and stupid policemen who have to have things worked out for them. Forget sleazy guys in crumpled raincoats and trilby hats, talking to cops as they would talk to a thug in a spit-and-sawdust pub. You don't walk into your local police station, and there isn't one, and announce your self-appointed role in one of their investigations. For one thing, modern administrative practices and the always popular hiding behind confidentiality, don't permit it. In the second, I don't even look like the acceptable type of amateur sleuth. Detective to you. You need to look like Miss Marple ..."

"Who's she?"

"An amateur detective. Agatha Christie."

"Who's she?"

"I just told you. Oh, she was a writer who wrote stories about an oldish lady who did amateur detective things. Ridiculous, but very enjoyable."

"Well, why can't you be like this Miss Marple?"

"She was old ...ish, and plain."

"Well, you're young...ish, and plain. Miss Marple couldn't have always been old."

Youngish and plain. One day, he was going to make someone very unhappy. A natural esteem-lowerer. A confidence-crusher. In the meantime, he wasn't doing much good for *her* self-esteem.

"So, what are you currently investigating?" asked the impervious one.

"Nothing just now. But something will turn up soon. It always does."

"So you just look at the local news until something suitable appears?"

"Not just the local news. The world news."

"So if someone is murdered in a far-off country, like …"

She could see him struggling. Clearly, world news and geography lessons had passed him by. She helped him out. "Venezuela? Ecuador? Lithuania?"

"Rovers had a player from Ecuador."

"What an incentive to find out where it is. Where is it?"

"I don't know. Africa?"

"South America."

Eric shrugged.

Charity resumed. "So, if someone in South America was killed, and it was a mystery, I'd try to work it out."

"From here."

"Yes. It's a hobby, not a job."

"What *is* your job?"

"I don't have one. I have an inheritance. Several, actually. A short burst of bad luck amongst some close, old, relations."

"Not bad luck for you. Sounds very suspicious. You should investigate yourself."

"Oh, no. I might find something incriminating." She looked at him thoughtfully. "How much money do you have, Eric?"

"I had eighty pounds in birthday money a couple of weeks ago. I … why?"

Eric was nervous again. Charity added to it.

"Just making conversation. Eighty pounds, you say?"

"Yes, but I soon spent it," he said hurriedly. "Hardly anything left."

"Did your mum give you some spending money for while you're with me?"

"No. She didn't give me anything."

"Really? Well, that's a poor show. Is she expecting me to pay for *everything*? She's spared the expense of three weeks of feeding you and washing your clothes, *and* three weeks pocket money."

"Yes. Write and tell her."

"And *that's* another thing. She didn't tell me where to find her in case of an emergency. She delivered you like a ticking bomb and ran for it."

"Perhaps she's confident there won't *be* an emergency."

Charity gave him an expression of profound doubt.

He winced. "You're probably right."

"And for good measure," added Charity. "She's probably gone to somewhere with a bad signal."

"At least that's what she'll say."

She pretended to be horrified. "Eric! That is not what a loved and loving son should say about his mother."

"Even if it's true?"

"Even if … it were true, which of course it isn't. Your mother and father are, well, they're, parents who love the child that they brought into the world."

"I know how they did it."

"Did what?" Now Charity was nervous.

"Brought me into the world, as you put it."

"Time for a change of subject," she said brightly. "I see you've managed to eat the toast and the shredded marmalade, so well done. Brush your teeth, and what do you say to a walk across the fields to the woods?"

"Is there any point in my saying anything?"

"Well, you could just say that it's a good idea that meets with your approval."

"But it doesn't."

"Well, it'll be good for you."

He gave her a long, hard look.

"Message received," Charity said. "You don't like things which are good for you. Well, you're probably not in a minority with that one. I know a lot of adults who don't like things that are good for them. Then they want pills to put right what the things that are bad for them have done. Brush your teeth, and we'll go for a walk. If you collapse from physical exhaustion or have a nervous breakdown, I'll hurry home and call an ambulance."

"Very funny."

"I try to be."

CHAPTER FOUR

Charity looked at the heap of things on her bed and said, "I apologise, Eric. You do not have a toothbrush, and you do not have a pair of shoes for walking through fields and woods. I can let you have a spare, still in the wrapper, toothbrush, but ..."

"The walk's off. And I was looking forward to it. I really did fancy a walk."

"And I'm not going to disappoint you, Eric. Before the walk, we'll pop out and buy some shoes."

"I couldn't put you to all that trouble and expense."

"You're clearly learning the language through adult insincerity. However, don't worry about it. The trouble and expense will be worth it to provide you with some fresh air and exercise."

"Oh," he said, contemplating defeat.

For a while, he walked along the road in morose contemplation, or morose vacancy. Charity couldn't decide which. He emanated sullen resentfulness, and every gesture suggested a determination to see only defects in the village.

She offered interesting items of information, historical, geographical and topographical, but to no avail. The frown was fixed, the jaw was set, the shoulders were hunched in support of his imagined weight of tedium.

As they approached the shops, she said, "We don't have much in the way of old-style shops or even new-style shops in the village, but what we do have is three charity shops."

"Were you named after them?"

"No. Well, yes, very indirectly, I suppose. Charity has existed for a very long time. But they're changing the names of the shops now, because people don't want charity."

"Aw, never mind. One day, someone will want you."

At least it was humour, of a sort. Anything was better than that moroseness. Was that the right word? She didn't like it, and invented a new word: morosity. Much better.

She pulled him into the first shop. "Right. Look for sturdy shoes or boots. Preferably, boots. No, obviously not those, Eric. Those are boots for a man with large feet. No, those are women's tennis shoes. Eric! Children's things are over there, in the children's section."

"Well, I don't know. I've never been in a junk shop before."

"It's not a junk shop."

"That's what mum calls them. She won't go in them. She says she doesn't want things that other people have had first."

"Be grateful that your father didn't have that policy."

"How about these? They light up."

"Oh, yes. If I lose you in the woods, I can find you easily. On the other hand, I might not want to. Try again. Sturdy, not pretty."

At the third shop, when they were both fed up, they found a pair which fitted.

"I hope no-one sees me in them," he said dismally.

"Unless you have discovered invisibility, you will be seen, at least until we leave the village. But try to understand this important point, Eric: *no-one will be interested in you*. They won't look at your feet, and they will be barely aware of the rest of you."

"What am I going to do with my other shoes?"

"Put them in the backpack."

That reminded him that he didn't like having the backpack. He tried to scowl at it, turning round. Charity put her hands in the volume magnification position and called, "It's behind you, Eric."

"So I have to lug a pair of shoes all round this walk?"

"I'm lugging the food, drinks, binoculars, plastic ponchos, first aid kit, and other things that we might need. Your backpack is currently empty. The addition of a pair of children's shoes is not a hardship."

"I'm a child."

"Oh, playing the child card now, after playing the superior male. At bedtime, you'll revert into a grown-up, as no doubt when you see me with a glass of wine."

"I've had wine. I like it."

"That proves my point. Well, little wine-drinker, you can manage to carry your shoes in your backpack."

She was very relieved when they turned into the narrow lane which led from the high street, leaving the shops and most of the people behind. She enjoyed being on the way to fields and trees, but the lane provided its own pleasure. The wild wood had its ancient, fundamental appeal, but the lane had its more recent appeal. It belonged to a recent past which she hadn't known. A time when suburban encroachment had gone only a little way, then stopped politely when it reached the great hordes of oak, sycamore and chestnut. Trees and cottages stood in a placid acceptance of each other, and the lane was the link between the two.

"Owww," cried Eric as he tripped over a stone and fell with a distinct thud on another stone. For good measure, he repeated the wail of pain.

"Good start," said Charity, removing her backpack. "But don't you worry about a little cut. I have my first aid kit."

"It's not a little cut, and it's bleeding."

"That's good. Bleeding cleans. But to be on the safe side, I'll put a little oinkment on it."

"Did you say 'oinkment'?"

"Yes. It's what pigs use."

"That's silly."

"I know. I like to be silly. I was much too sensible as a child."

She put on a plaster and said, "Now, the important thing, until you are used to it, is to walk looking generally down. There are stones of many sizes and shapes, sneaky brambles and *roots*. They are big trippers. The biggest bad guys of tripping."

"And this is supposed to be good for me? And I'm supposed to enjoy it?"

"The benefits from it are available for you. If you reject them, then you won't have them. It's your choice."

"Coming out here isn't."

"No, but that isn't relevant. What I want you to understand is that you have control over what this is. If it's boring, it's because you've allowed it to be boring."

"That's daft. Boring is boring."

"No! What do you think of chess."

"That's as boring as this is."

"But to two people playing chess…"

Two stiles and two fields later, she stopped and said, "Simple things to look for. Summer mushrooms. Wild celery. Rosehips. Elderflowers. And gather as many dandelions as you want."

"They're weeds."

"They're herbs. Very good for you."

"Mushrooms are poisonous, except shop ones."

"Nonsense. Lots of delicious mushrooms grow wild. But some are very poisonous. A quarter of a Death Cap would kill you. Horribly."

"Well, you keep all your wild stuff well away from me."

"That reminds me of an old joke. A man is commiserating with a woman about the death of her two husbands. He asks what the first one died of. She replies, 'Posionous mushrooms.' The man says, 'Oh, dear. What did the second one die of?' She replies, 'A blow on the head.' The man says, 'Oh, dear. How did that happen?' The woman replies, 'Wouldn't eat his mushrooms.'"

"That's silly."

"Of course it is. But it made you smile."

"Hmm, no it didn't make me smile. I smiled because you told me a joke and wanted me to smile."

"Well, Eric, perhaps the best smile isn't one which shows someone's happiness, but one which tries to make someone else happy."

"Uh," was the non-committal reply.

There was an odd silence for a little while, until they entered the woodland of trees and ferns.

"The wild wood," Charity said with relish.

Eric frowned. But what else is there besides mushrooms which might kill me, celery, which I hate, and weeds?"

"Lots of things. Everything is interesting."

"Interesting for me."

"Oh, I don't know. Perhaps we'll find a dead person."

"Oh, cool."

She stopped and said, "Just listen to the sounds of the wood."

"Look, up there." She pointed upwards and stepped back, tripped and toppled backwards.

Eric thought it was hilarious. Seeing Charity's puzzled expression, he said, "Oh, come on. It was funny."

"Hmm? Oh, yes it was. Until I saw this."

"What is it?"

"A dead person."

CHAPTER FIVE

Charity held up her hand, and said, "No! Stay there."

Eric grumbled, "I want to see the dead person. I haven't seen one before."

"Eric! Not only do I not want to satisfy your macabre cravings, I don't want you clumping over the crime scene before I check the immediate area for footprints, or other evidence. It might not even be the crime scene. Look at those ferns. The body might have been dragged here after the murder."

"Ooh, yes. Then this would be crime scene B, assuming it's a crime to deposit a dead body."

"Eric, shut up while I examine the body without touching it. For all I know it might not even be a oh, yes it is."

"Knife or gunshot?"

"Knife."

"How do you …?"

"Still in him."

"Check it for fingerprints."

"I brought a first aid kit, not a portable forensic kit. Besides, I mustn't touch anything, or the police would have a collective fit. They'd probably arrest me instead."

She looked down again. The man was wearing a waistcoat, and a tiny bit of paper stuck out of one of the small, tight pockets. Oh, temptation. She could look and put it back. How could anyone know? Would she leave fingerprints on the paper? Surely not.

"Eric," she said. "If you want to be useful, without encroaching on the crime scene, just investigate the grass and ferns over there, looking for the signs of a dragged body."

"Right." Enjoying his new role, he went off, peering, with a sleuthily bent back.

"Of course," he called, "it could be suicide."

The great distractor. "What?" Charity snapped. "Stabbed himself in the chest?"

"Like a Japanese suicide."

"They don't stab themselves in the chest. They ... do it somewhere else. And he isn't Japanese. And it's right up ... well, pushed right in. Now, just do what I've asked you to do."

Very carefully, she gripped the piece of paper delicately between her finger and thumb and gently pulled.

Tom.

I'm in Dryer's Wood. By the big Oak. I'll explain.

Suzy.

She closed the piece of paper and carefully inserted it in the waistcoat pocket, leaving the slight projection as before.

"Yes," called Eric as he returned. "Definitely dragging

signs. But why did he leave the knife in him? Isn't it evidence?"

"Exactly what I was thinking, Eric. But then I thought of the answer."

"Oh. What?"

"He was interrupted. By people arriving."

"Oh, yes, that's a thought. That …oh. We're people arriving."

"Yes. And I think we'd better depart."

Eric spoke in a stage whisper, out of the side of his mouth. "Don't look, but I think I can see him."

"Where?"

"In those bushes, between the two thin trees. Don't look!"

Of course she looked.

The face was all that she could see.

Watching and waiting.

For them to leave, or just turn their backs to leave?

"Right," she said. "Walk briskly for a little way, then run."

"I'm not a fast runner."

"You will be." She was already leading him away.

She didn't want to look back, but she also didn't want to wait for the thudding and panting of pursuit.

She looked.

He was walking quickly.

He was starting to run.

"Run, Eric!"

She was right about his necessity running. He was faster than she was. He was a slouch, she was a walker, but they were both hurtling.

So was the man behind them.

Faster than both of them.

Could they stay out of reach, at least until they reached the open fields, then the lane?

Of course not. He was …gone.

He'd disappeared.

To the side? A short cut? About to leap out ahead?

But why do that?

She slowly braked, pulling Eric until they both stood still, gasping and looking round.

"Why?" she said.

"Perhaps to make us stop running, making it easier for him."

"That sudden exercise has set your brain working. Excellent suggestion. It doesn't make me feel better, but well done."

Now that they had stopped, she looked around for a suitable stick for a weapon. After a couple of annoyingly brittle ones, she found one which should be capable of doing damage.

All the time that she was searching and testing, she was looking around, and up, nervously expecting him to drop from a tree.

After much grunting, Eric pulled off a long strand of bramble. "A spiky whip," he said with satisfaction.

"Well done, Eric. Together, we can defeat the enemy. I'll bonk him on the head and you tear his eyes out."

That prospect impressed him.

"Right. Let's proceed with brisk caution."

"What does that mean?"

"I'm not sure."

CHAPTER SIX

Clutching their improvised weapons, walking quickly, they left the wood, crossed the fields, slowed down along the lane, and emerged, with big sighs of relief, into the high street. It looked reassuringly, comfortably, dull.

"Never underestimate simple ordinariness," Charity said. "Most of the world would gladly settle for this."

"Well, I'm glad we're safe," Eric partially agreed.

"That, too, is what most of the world desires."

"What now? Home for some food?"

"A snack, then off to Luckham to report this."

"Oh, you don't need me. I'll be fine on my own."

"Probably, but one doesn't take risks nowadays. If I were to leave you on your own and come back to find you'd poisoned yourself or burnt yourself to death, I'd be in so much trouble. Everyone would be moaning at me. I'd probably be charged with neglect. No, I can't risk that, Eric. You'll have to come with me. On the way back, remind me to buy some jelly marmalade for you."

After Eric had condescended to eat some cheese and

chutney sandwiches, Charity reversed the car onto the road. She kept stopping to check that Eric wasn't lying down behind the car. She admitted to herself that she was over-wrought, and having a bit of a reaction to the earlier event, but she wasn't in the mood for taking any chances.

It was only six miles to Luckham, but that was ample space for two sets of long roadworks. "This must have been very frustrating for your parents," she murmured.

When they eventually reached the town, she parked in the supermarket car park. She was going to buy a lot of stuff if anyone objected; but first, she had important business at the police station.

She walked up the steps as a policeman hurried down them. He said, "We close at three on a Thursday."

"Close? I don't want to *buy* anything. I wish to report something."

"We have an online link for reporting things."

"But I'm here, not online."

"If you want to complain about cuts and reduced services, you're welcome to write to your councillor."

"Perhaps I shall. But right now, I have an urgent need for a policeman. A real one. Not a copbot."

He sighed as though all the troubles of the world had descended on him at the same time that it began to rain. "What is it?" he asked with a corresponding brusqueness.

Charity looked at him for a moment in silent disap-proval, then said, "I wish to report a murder."

"Oh, yes," he said slowly. "Whose?"

"*I* don't know. My ... temporary nephew and I went for a walk in the woods, and we found a dead body. Then a man pursued us, until he disappeared."

"Disappeared?"

"Yes. Please don't do that tangent thing. That can come in the longer, slower version. The statement or whatever it is. In the meantime, you need to investigate."

"Are you sure this person was dead? Not just drunk or fooling around?"

"He had a knife in his chest, and blood all over his front."

Another big, martyred sigh. "Well, I can't do anything right now. I'll pass it on, and someone will come out to interview you. They might want you to take them to this dead body."

"Oh, they might? Well, I look forward to a visit."

"Who are you, and where do you live?"

She told him. He said, "Well, as I said …don't know when it'll be."

"Well, thank you for your … help. Come on, Eric."

Even Eric waited until they had left the police forecourt before saying, "What an idiot. After all we've done. Found a body for them and reported it. You'd think they'd be grateful."

"Yes, you would. All this puts your food preferences in perspective. Let's enjoy ourselves in the supermarket. What do you like besides baked beans?"

"I like curry. Curried baked beans are nice."

"Anything a bit less turbulent? Doughnuts? Pizza? Fish and chips?"

"Yes, I like all those, too."

"In that case, Eric, I shall load up with them. I'll beat those beans with pastry and batter."

"What?"

"Take no notice. I'm rambling. And after the excitement of today, I think I'll join you in the comforting stodge."

They walked over to the supermarket. Charity pulled out a trolley and said, "Pick up a basket when we go in. You can choose your favourite things to eat, drink and watch, and we'll meet at the till, and you can put your selection in the trolley. If we went round together, I'd be disapproving of what you wanted and you'd be disapproving of what I wanted."

"I wouldn't …"

"Broccoli, Eric."

"I'll go and find the frozen peas."

"You're like a miniature husband."

"I thought you didn't want a husband."

"Ah, well, that's because you can't hand a husband back to his parents after three weeks."

While Eric loaded his basket in the freezer section, Charity did her best to find the least offensive vegetables. She settled for potatoes, carrots and a swede. She could add strongly flavoured things to please Eric. Passing Eric, and glancing in his basket, she saw that he was choosing the worst pizzas available, and she picked some Margaritas for herself. And with a dazzle of inspiration, she added the ingredients for a home-made pizza, going back to the vegetable section for peppers and mushrooms, and the best garlics that she could find. She would show him that a pizza can be healthy. Sort of.

Next was shredless marmalade, different flavours, and shredless, seedless jam, different flavours. And smooth peanut butter. Everyone likes peanut butter. Except those who don't. Some sugary cereals. And she pulled cakes off the shelves as though she were doing a robbery.

When they met and merged, she joined the shortest

queue. After three seconds, Eric said, "Can I wait in the car?"

"I expect so, but you'd have to ask for my permission first."

"I just did."

"No. You asked whether you are capable of waiting in the car."

Eric groaned. That old thing, so popular with old people. "*May* I wait in the car?"

"Yes. Here's the key. You …"

"I know what to do. My friend Alec's mum has one the same as yours for popping to the shops and things. It's her runaround."

"Is it? Well, my mechanical marvel, go and make yourself comfortable. Don't touch anything. No, please don't say it. You may touch the passenger seat for the purpose of sitting in it. Restrain your curiosity. Don't fiddle and twiddle. Don't play car driver. Wait patiently in comfort while I stand and wait patiently in this stationary queue."

"You picked the wrong one."

"I always pick the wrong one. I could prove it to you by going to another queue and making that one stationary."

"I'll go and wait in the car."

"Good idea."

She looked up the line to see what was causing, or extending, the creeping delay. Oh, coupons. Or vouchers. The cashier had three piles, presumably acceptable, out of date, and not even this supermarket. What a day. Eric, a murder, a pursuing maniac, an annoying policeman, and a woman with coupons. And more Eric to come. Much more. Three weeks of it.

She muttered, "Curried baked beans."

"Pardon?" said the man in front of her.

"Sorry," she said. "Just thinking of things while I stand here."

When the man had turned away, she thought that curried baked beans would be a good exclamation or a huffy response. Oh … curried baked beans!

The coupons had been sorted, the payment had been made. Now, the woman started packing, carefully into bags.

Oh, curried baked beans!

CHAPTER SEVEN

Of course, the police arrived, with a vigorous knocking on the door, just as Charity was serving the evening meal. She had cooked it carefully to ensure that both pizzas were ready together.

"It must be the police. No-one else knocks like that."

"Tell them to come back later."

"In the first place, you don't say that to police people. Well, I don't. I'm old-fashioned. I'm frightened of them. In the second place, you might remember that I was the one who requested very earnestly for the police to be interested in our murder, so to speak."

She was already moving towards the door. When she opened it, two police officers stood there.

"Miss Shields?"

Why did they always make it sound as though you shouldn't be?

"Yes. Is it about the murder?"

"Well, let's not run ahead of ourselves. We have had a

report of something suspicious, and we need to verify that, if we can. First, I am Constable Maikes, and this is Constable Wilkins."

"Hello. Thank you for calling."

"We are following a procedure for dealing with a report of this kind."

"Right, Well, you tell me what you want me to do, and I'll do it."

"Later, we shall ask you for a detailed statement of what occurred, but first we'd like you to show us the body."

"Of course. Yes. I'll just put my hat and boots on. They're rather dirty." She pointed at them by their feet. "Have you a newspaper or something in your car?"

"Don't worry about it, said Constable Wilkins. "We're in rather a hurry."

"Oh. Another one after mine? Not another murder, I hope."

She realised that she was nervously babbling, started to explain that she was nervously babbling, then went inside for her coat.

And Eric. "You must come, Eric."

He thought about it and said, "I'd like to, really, but it's too many people now. I think I'll just stay here and watch something on my iPad."

"Eric! How many more times? I will not be blamed for your death."

There was a cough outside the open front door. She frowned at Eric. "Put your jacket and shoes on, and let's do this before it's dark."

As she led him out she said to the waiting officers, This is my ...oh, I don't know what he is. He's the son of an old friend. They've gone off for three weeks."

"Where to?"

"I don't know. They rushed off. Did they tell you, Eric?"

"Somewhere hot and quiet where children aren't allowed."

"That narrows it down," Charity said. "Any old detective should be able to work that one out."

"Shall we go?" said Constable Wilkins.

"Yes. Right," she said, bending down to ease her feet into her boots.

When she opened the car door, Charity said, "Did they tell you that it's across two fields, in the middle, roughly speaking, of a wood?"

"The report that was passed to us wasn't specific about that. We'll just drive as far as we can and walk the rest of the way."

They drove into town, and just as Charity was starting to say that they needed to turn right and stop, the GPS told them to keep going. Shortly after, to her disappointment and disgust, she became aware that what she thought of as the wild wood was a small wood, on the other side of which was a lane, with tracks which showed frequent use by motor vehicles.

But if cars could come this close, it would make it much easier to take a body into the wood. She didn't say anything. It looked as though police officers were like general practitioners in not wanting people to work things out for themselves.

When the car stopped, Wilkins said, "Do you think you can find the location from this side?"

"Probably. But I need to be in the wood to see."

"Right. Let's go."

A narrow ditch and a low fence were the only obstacles,

and a few minutes steady striding took them to an area
which Charity recognised. "Just through here and bear
right," she said, ducking under some low branches. "Here
…it …"

"What's that?" Maikes was enjoying it.

"It seems to be a dead sheep."

"*Seems* to be? All that wool is a pretty good indication of
what it is."

She walked about, darting this way and that, not believing, but knowing. *This* was the place. This *was* the place.

She looked at the police officers, who wore invisible
smirks on their stern faces. "You don't really think that I
mistook a dead sheep for a dead human, do you?"

"Well, er …"

"We're not, er …"

"How far away were you?" asked Wilkins.

Charity answered slowly. "I knelt beside the body."

"Did you do the customary checks to confirm that the
er, person was dead?"

"No. In accordance with the rule about not touching
anything, I didn't."

"So," said Maikes, "the person could have walked away,
or been helped away."

Charity rubbed her face and said, "Which one are you
going for, the dead person who turned out to be a dead
sheep, or the person who wasn't dead and walked away?"

"Either way," said Wilkins, "what we don't have is a
dead person. And we've been dragged out to see a dead
person."

"You *haven't* been dragged …." She stopped, reminded,
and turned away.

Eric joined her and said, "It's not as squashed down as it was."

"No." Charity spun round. "How did the sheep die?"

"How do we know?" Maikes squawked. "What's that to do with it? Are you changing your story to a murdered sheep?"

Charity walked round the sheep and said, "No sign of wounds, so the cause of death becomes important." She looked round. "Where's its flock. The nearest sheep farm that I know round here is about two miles away."

Wilkins did a big shrug and said, "Well, there's your answer. This one became separated, wandered off and died."

"*Of what?*"

"That's what we don't know. Perhaps it was ill with a disease or some other sheep ailment, and wandered off to die."

"Two miles? This is a sheep, not a mythical elephant."

"Look," said Wilkins. "You're obviously excited and upset about whatever it was that happened, or didn't happen, but the important fact is that you reported a murder, and in the place where you said the dead body was, there is a dead sheep. Now, my colleague and I are required to write a report. It's important, for us at least, that our report doesn't contain any further ... displays of ... well, eccentricity. Does that make sense?"

"I understand what you are saying."

Maikes said, "In that case, shall we be taking you home?"

"Yes, but please don't treat me as though I'm a confused old lady. And please wait for just a few seconds."

She walked away from the sheep into the thicker part of

the wood, looking closely at the ground. Eric followed her. "What are you looking for, Charity?"

She put a hand on each of his shoulders. "Exactly what I was hoping to find, Eric." She put a finger to her lips. "I'll tell you when we're back home."

CHAPTER EIGHT

"They weren't very helpful," said Eric when they were home again.

"They weren't helpful at all," Charity replied. "Cold pizza?"

Eric shrugged. "Yeah, fine. What are you going to tell me later, which is now?"

"Right. Well, while the police were having their fun with me, I did what they should have been doing. I *thought*. You and I know there was a dead person there."

"Assuming it was the right place."

"It *was*. You were there. Both times."

"Yes, but I'm not very good with details. One bit of a wood looks the same as any other to me."

"Okay. I'll take you off the witness stand, but we'll keep going. There was a dead person. Then, there wasn't. Instead, there was a dead sheep. Therefore, the human body was removed and the sheep's body was delivered. In a real wild wood, that would have been very difficult. But now I know that it isn't as big as I thought, and there's a lane passing close by, it becomes much less difficult. So, I thought, how would I do it? A very good way of working these things out. And that's why I went off looking for an indication. And there was."

"Which was?"

"The track of a wheelbarrow. Easy to recognise. What else has one wheel?"

"A monocycle."

"How would you carry a sheep on a monocycle?"

"I didn't say anyone would. You asked what else has one wheel."

"Fair enough. So, a wheelbarrow was used. One dead body out, another dead body in. Any questions so far?"

"How did whoever it was find a dead sheep?"

"Perhaps someone who had access to sheep, the means of removing a sheep, and a vehicle big enough to carry a wheelbarrow. And, before you ask, did you know that sheep that are stuck on their backs, die? So, it might not have been necessary to kill that sheep, which had no visible wounds. It might have died naturally, so to speak. So put all those together, and what does it suggest?"

"*I* don't know."

"Oh, *think*, boy. Access to sheep, especially one which has recently died, large wheelbarrow, large vehicles, and I mentioned a sheep farm a couple of miles away."

The penny dropped with a loud clunk. "Oh, a farmer."

"Yes." She sat back triumphantly.

"So what are you going to do next?"

"Observe and make enquiries?"

"How?"

"I don't know. One important aspect of this is the note."

"Which note?"

"There was a note on the dead body. I took it out, read it and put it back. I didn't tell the police in case that was against the not touching rule, and because, well, they were being so unhelpful, and I thought it would be a waste of valuable evidence to tell them."

"What did the note say?"

Charity nodded a few times as she remembered. "'Tom. I'm in Dryer's Wood. By the big oak. I'll explain. Suzy.'"

"Who's Tom? Who's Suzy?"

"I don't know. I don't mingle much. I don't have a social life. I've never joined any of the local groups."

"It might have helped if you had."

"Yes, I realise that. But all my investigation work, if you can call it that, was hypothetical, theoretical, little more than ponderings, possible material for a book which I might write one day."

"What's it about?"

"I haven't written it. I haven't even thought of a plot."

"You have one now. The plot has come to you."

She grinned. "Good boy, Eric. Life is all about opportunities and what you do with them. We'll solve the case, and I'll write it."

"Will you put me in it?"

"Well, are you going to be my assistant through this investigation, or at least until your parents return?"

"Oh, yes."

"Then of course you'll be in it. You'll be my Watson."

"Who?"

"When we're not investigating, I'm going to start your training with some interesting reading."

"Oh?"

"Don't worry, Eric. It won't hurt."

CHAPTER NINE

"Now, are you clear about it?" Charity asked as the car approached the farm.

"Yes."

"Good."

After an early success with sugary cereals and various jelly stuffs on toast, she had driven to the lane on the other side of the wood, and gone back to the scene of the missing crime. First, she looked in the lane for a wheelbarrow track.

"Here?" called Eric, looking down eagerly.

"Well done," Charity said.

"But then it stops."

She leapt over the ditch. "And resumes over here. Obviously, a short plank was used. A wheelbarrow containing a dead sheep would be very difficult to manoeuvre across a ditch. And that weight is going to give us the big advantage of a clear track.

She scuttled off, peering. Eric followed her, doing the same, confirming. The track frequently disappeared over rough ground, but soon reappeared. Once, it did a detour round a tight cluster of trees, but they were keenly following and never lost it for long. And when it led precisely to the spot where Charity had first found it, almost at the sheep, she exclaimed, "We've done it, Eric!"

With no police in attendance, she pulled at the dead sheep, looking for any signs of violence. Then she did a final check to confirm that there were no indications that the sheep had walked there.

"I thought we'd just proved it hadn't walked here," Eric said.

"I'm just wrapping it all up, or whatever the expression is. We have the obvious evidence of the dead sheep with no marks of violence; we have the wheelbarrow track; and we have the lack of hoof prints. So, there is no scope for an objector to say, 'But…'. All the necessary information is there."

"Brilliant."

"Thank you. And now for the next step, which might be a complete failure."

"What's that?"

"Visit the farmer. Come on."

The lane was narrow and bendy, and it became steadily more narrow and more bendy, then dwindled into a rough track. The car bumped and slithered along into the even rougher yard. She stopped the car, but left the engine running.

"Why are we waiting?" asked Eric.

"For the inevitable barking dogs, followed by the inevitable barking farmer, unless he's out doing things with his sheep. Ah, here come the dogs."

"And here comes the farmer."

She wound down her window as a chunky-looking man

in a check jacket and corduroy trousers walked slowly towards them.

"Help you?" he said.

"Morning," Charity replied affably. "Couple of things. There's a dead sheep over in the wood. I thought it might be one of yours."

"I know about that. Going to move it later."

"And my nephew here is keen on doing farming in some form when he's old enough. I thought you might be able, and willing, to show him around."

"No. Not a chance. Much too busy. And you don't just let strangers wander round your farm nowadays. Health and Safety, insurance, all that red tape stuff. You'd have to arrange something with a specialist group."

"Ah. Good points. I should have thought." After some nodding, she said, "Poor old sheep, wandering all that way. No signs of injury. Died of exhaustion, do you think?"

"Probably. I'll know more when I collect it."

"It will take some shifting, through the trees and bushes."

"I'll manage. Don't you worry about that."

"You know where it is, then?"

"Yes. I know all about it. Nothing for you to worry about."

His tone was becoming sharper. It was clear that he wanted her to go, now.

"Right. Thank you," she said, still managing to sound pleasant. She turned the car round, waving as she drove away, noting the sour expression and lack of response.

Eric said, "I don't like him."

"On the basis of that short meeting, neither do I."

"So is he the murderer?"

"Eric, we must gather our information and not rush to decisions. And we must put to one side his unpleasant personality. Being unpleasant doesn't make you a murderer. However, based on the information that we've gathered so far, and the connection between the dead body removal and the sheep replacement, I strongly suspect his involvement."

"So he might be an accomplice."

"That's right. But no making the facts fit theories. We need more information."

"How are you going to do that?"

"I think this case requires the supreme act from me. I'm going to be sociable. In fact, I shall need to be Hamingdon's most sociable member. I am going to join things. I am going to visit pubs. I shall attend services at the church. And I shall listen for any mentions of Tom and Suzy. Together or separately."

She stopped to ponder. "Of course, one big bit of information that I don't have is the name of the dead person."

"Won't the police … well, eventually, find out about it, and then it would be in the local paper, that sort of thing."

"But the police might continue not knowing about the dead person."

"But surely someone will be reported as missing."

"He might not be from round here. And the police will always take the view that without a body, missing does not equal murdered."

"Well, after what you told them, they should be able to put two and two together."

"They will. And make three. They don't want a murder in Hamingdon. They want people to dine in The Royal Oak, stay at Netterton's Hotel, fish on the Orr, all that sort of thing. They don't want people avoiding the place or moping around looking at crime scenes."

"You might be famous. The one who found the body. The one who solved the crime. You could be the murder tour guide."

"Let's stick with trying to solve the crime. First, let's see what groups round here are suitable for me."

She turned on the computer and opened the Hamingdon home page.

"There probably aren't any suitable for you. I mean, you're … you."

"What does that mean?"

"Well, you're not the sort to fit in with other people."

"What? You think I'm odd?"

"No, stupid."

"You think I'm stupid?"

"No! I was calling you stupid. You're … just, well, different."

"We'll come back to the 'stupid' another time. So, you see me as too different to fit in with other people."

"Oh, I didn't mean anything *bad*. No. I … it's just that I don't see you sitting in group things talking about insects or local history, or making pots or whatever."

"Well, you might have a point. But *my* point is that I must do something of the sort if I'm to find out about people."

"Okay. I can see that. I just think you'll be struggling finding the right things for you."

"And for you, dear."

"*What?*"

Charity smiled sweetly. "I'm in charge of you. I must

take good care of you. It's in the unwritten contract that your mother didn't have time to sign."

"You can trust me on my own."

"I *can*, but I *may* not, must not, and won't. Besides, as my assistant, I shall require your support, and your observational skills. Who knows? One of these groups might contain ... *the murderer*."

"Oh, all right."

"Good."

"But I'm not making pottery. I have enough of that stuff at school."

"Pottery at school. Lucky boy. However, pottery doesn't appeal to me either. I'm not very good with my hands. Let's see what there is. Local history. That's one. That will do for now. Don't groan. If I'd been in that group, I might have known that the wild wood finishes a short way beyond where we found the body."

Eric's groans had settled into a low whine.

"Look," Charity said. "While I'm busy participating, you, my assistant, can skip the boring stuff and concentrate on watching people, and listening to their private conversations. You enjoy eavesdropping don't you? Earwigging? Listening to what people don't want you to hear?"

Suspicion and enthusiasm vied for control of Eric, and it showed in his face. Charity concealed her amusement, and regarded him earnestly.

"Well," he said, "I'd rather stay home, but I suppose you need my help. I can't leave you to do it on your own. Okay."

"Excellent. You are now free to roam around the house while I do my online applications."

"Anything to eat?"

"My plan, part of the mingling plan, is to treat you to lunch out. But if you think you can't last that long, there are some killer snacks, especially for you, in the top right cupboard. One only. You'll need to ..."

"I know how to take stuff out of top cupboards. Been doing it for years."

She heard him hoisting himself up with a clatter and opening the cupboard. After a brief rummage, the cupboard was closed, and he dropped to the floor with a clump.

Ignoring the rustling sounds of the bag-opening, she started to tap.

"D'oh!"

"What is it?"

"The stupid bag suddenly tore open. They've gone all over the floor. Okay, I'll scoop them up. Do you have a bowl, like a cereal bowl."

"I have some bowls which really are cereal bowls. Bottom left cupboard."

"Where's that? Oh, right."

She closed her eyes when she heard crockery breaking. "What are you doing, Eric?"

"Sorry. They weren't stacked well. A couple slid out. They're okay now."

"How are they okay?"

"I meant the others are okay. Right. It's all under control here. You do your thing in there."

She made herself concentrate as she tapped away, registering with passwords, answering questions, and trying to convey enthusiasm, which she certainly wasn't feeling.

"Right," she said when she turned off the computer. "Do you have enough appetite left for a burger and chips?"

"Aw, yes."

"In that case, we shall go to the local pub, where in addition to extravagant food for rich gourmands, they have hedged their bets with the provision of more prosaic food for the lower end of the market, represented on this occasion by you."

"What?"

"Never mind. Toilet and wash your hands."

CHAPTER TEN

"All ordered," Charity said, after a long wait at the food queue.

"Did you ask for the gherkin?"

"No. This isn't a fast food place. It will be a real burger."

"But I like ..."

"Don't say it, Eric. Not company names, not company products, not things that go in the products. I have paid a lot of money for this. I don't want you to lift off the top and inspect it for gherkins, and mutter about the ones you like all through the meal and grumble because there isn't a plastic toy. Just settle back and enjoy it. And don't forget to observe. I have to go and buy the drinks now."

She hated the strict organisation of the modern pub, with its separate food and drink queues, its surly 'What's your table number?' service, pay by card in advance, eat your meal and clear off. But at least they could eat their meal and clear off.

When the barman brought the drinks, she said, "Has Tom been in?"

"Tom?"

"Yes, Tom."

"Hasn't been in for a while," said the woman to his right, not really joining the brief conversation. The barman shrugged, and Charity said, "Thanks," in the direction of the woman.

As she turned to take the drinks back, a voice to her left said, "Is your name Suzy?"

Charity wondered how things would develop if she replied that she was, but there was too much potential for complications, and even danger.

"No," she answered. "I think she's a friend of Tom's."

"She is, but you aren't." A statement question.

"No."

"I wondered when I heard you asking about him."

"I hadn't seen him around for a few days, and just thought I'd ask."

"Ah, I see. You don't want him for anything particular, then?"

She decided to turn the tables. "Do *you* know Tom?"

"In a way."

"What way is that?"

"Oh … business acquaintance."

"Oh. Does he owe you money?"

"No. He owes me a wife."

At the edge of her vision, Charity saw their food being delivered. It was time to be decisive. She said, "I have to go back to my nephew. Our food has arrived. Perhaps we could discuss this, sometime."

He didn't seem very keen, which she thought was a good point, regarding safety; but he wasn't dismissive about the suggestion. After a few moments of thought, he said,

"I'm sure that you won't feel like discussing anything with a stranger after a Royal Oak burger and chips. How about an early drink, say six o'clock?"

"Yes. I shall have my nephew with me. Also, my assistant. That's not another person. That's my nephew. I promoted him."

The man smiled. "Well, Miss, or Mrs, or Ms…"

"Charity Shields," she replied, not choosing a title.

"Bernie Pocket. I look forward to a chat at six. Enjoy your meal."

Back at the table, she sat down and said, "Thank you for waiting, but it would have been more impressive if you weren't poised over your food like a vampire."

"I'm hungry."

"Off you go, then."

Eric loaded his mouth with burger, bun and chips, then said, "Oozaman?"

"A stranger who seems to know Tom. We're going to meet him here at six."

"What about?"

"I don't know. But hopefully it will throw some light on the Tom and Suzy mystery. Now, stop talking and enjoy your food."

Her veggie burger wasn't a reluctant menu alternative to spread the pub's appeal, and she enjoyed it. After a while, she began to struggle with the chips, and glanced across at Eric. He looked at her and said, "It's big, isn't it?"

"I suppose I should have asked for the children's menu," she said. "I really didn't think of it. It doesn't really go with your being my assistant."

"No, this is fine," he said earnestly. "Really. I'm just not used to so much."

"Neither am I. I'm struggling, too. Relax and enjoy it until you're stuffed."

"I'm stuffed."

"So am I. It probably won't keep well, but I always have sandwich bags in case of, well, anything. We'll wrap it as well as we can in the serviettes, and put it in these, and we might want it for supper."

By the time they had wrapped the food and inserted it into the bags, it wasn't looking likely that it would be wanted for supper.

"I'm thirsty now," Eric said.

"Plenty to drink at home, at much lower prices. And those people at the bar look like hungry table vultures, desperate for us to leave. Watch them when we slowly stand, and I check that we haven't left anything behind, and then I tell you to check."

"They're already starting to edge forward, and someone just slid off a stool."

"Menacingly, like a predator?"

"Yes."

"Right. Is that everything? Check that you haven't left anything."

Eric was doing his bit, turning round twice, patting his pocket, looking under the table. Charity tapped him. "Okay, Eric. They're starting to look dangerous. Time to leave."

Outside, they laughed, then walked briskly home.

"What are we going to do this afternoon?" Eric asked.

"After you have done one thing, I suggest that you relax with your electronic games."

"Oh? What's the one thing?"

"A little bit of reading."

"Auugghow. Really?"

"Yes. Not a lot. A story."

"What's it about?"

"Murder, treasure, and detection."

"Oh, it's that one you mentioned, isn't it?"

"That's right. Read a few pages, then stop if you want. It's just a small beginning."

"Stop when I want?"

"After a few pages. Yes. Then you may scurry back to the safety of your games."

"What are you going to do?"

"A little cleaning, which is important with you dropping food on the floor and eating it. Then, a little research, which I should have done long ago. If I had looked at the satellite views for this area, I'd have seen the extent of the wild wood."

"But you do know now."

"Now I know that people are removing things from the wood, and bringing other things *to* the wood, I want to have a look at the area, looking especially at the various routes."

"I could look with you."

"If you prefer that instead of playing your games, fine."

"I meant instead of reading a book."

She stopped and swung him round to face her. "Eric! If you are going to be a valuable assistant, you *must* have a brain which is constantly being used and exercised."

"But what does reading an old book have to do with that?"

"Books provide the fuel on which the brain runs."

"Did you make that up?"

"Yes. But I'm sure that others have said similar things.

And this book will help you in your work with me. It's like a training manual, but with pleasure."

"Okay."

They were soon home. She set Eric in position with his book, feeling like a nurse with an old patient, did some housework in her usual frivolous way, trying to keep tension out of it, then settled back at her computer.

As it whirred itself into starting mode, she listened. Not a sound. What did it mean when you left an eleven year old boy with a book which he didn't want to read? She decided to leave him in his silence. If she checked on him, he might say, "Oh, I'd like a drink if you don't mind. All this reading is making me thirsty. I'd better have a break."

She went straight into satellite views of her area, down, down, down, then back up one because the annoying thing was blurred when she went too close. How were you supposed to spy on people when it kept blurring? But with some hard staring, and taking the view up for clarity, then down, then back, she could convert what seemed to be into what probably was. From the bottom field of the sheep farm, there seemed to be a gate, and a track which led to a bend in the lane which led past the wild wood. In other words, a very convenient short cut.

Information. Another tiny item which might have no significance, until combined with a lot of other items.

She drifted for a while, looking at her own house, then going off to look at other places. When she went to street view, going steadily from curious to nosey, she knew that it was time to stop before her brain settled into the sludgey state.

Was there anything else while she was at the computer? No point in entering 'Tom' or 'Suzy'. But she did. As expected, pages of entries about actors, pop stars, models, and a famous cartoon cat.

No, she could search and conjecture away, but it would be pointless.

She needed to wait for what Bernie Pocket was going to provide.

She suspected that it was going to be very important.

CHAPTER ELEVEN

"So," Charity said, trying to sound confident, "what is this about Tom?"

"How do you know him?" asked Bernie, going straight to the question which Charity didn't want him to ask.

"He used to come here, often."

"That doesn't really answer my question."

"You didn't answer mine. You invited me here to discuss him. The ball is in your court."

He tilted his head. "Okay. I accept that. But I'm being careful because I'm worried about Tom, and my wife."

"Is that 'Tom and my wife' or 'Tom comma and my wife'?"

"Comma."

"Are Tom and your wife having an affair?"

"Yes. So, I believe. A week or so ago, she went off, leaving a note which said something about starting again. No address. Changed telephone number. A complete cut-off. I haven't heard from her since then."

"What has that to do with Tom?"

"Well, that was just my putting things together. She kept going out, and at the same time, Tom kept doing the same. Meeting someone for lunches."

"Who is Suzy?"

"A mystery woman. On the other hand, perhaps not, He always described her as a friend."

"Does Tom have a wife?"

"Divorced."

"Right. And you were business associates."

"Partners, actually. Joint owners of a building firm in Luckham. PH Developments. Tom Henry is, was, the builder, I am the marketing manager. Not a very good one, I'm the first to admit. I just go around being nice, and gently persuasive."

She was aware that she was doing all the pumping, but she didn't want to be the pumpee. How much should she tell this man? The dead body? The note? Didn't that suggest that the dead man was Tom?

He seemed to read her thoughts. "Your turn. You know Tom, but you seem to know almost nothing about him. You seem to know of someone called Suzy, but again, nothing about her."

Charity showed that she understood, took a deep breath, and said nothing. After another deep breath, she said, "My assistant and I went for a walk in the local wood. We found a dead man, with a knife in his chest. He was wearing a waistcoat."

She heard Bernie inhale strongly.

"In the waistcoat, there was a slip of paper, which said, 'Tom, I'm in Dyer's Wood. By the big oak. I'll explain. Suzy.'"

She paused. Bernie said, "Go on."

"With much effort, I persuaded the police to go out to look at the body. They parked in a lane which leads to a sheep farm. I led them to the spot. There was no human body. Instead, there was a dead sheep."

Bernie put his face through a few ruminative contortions, then asked, "Any sign of what had happened?"

"No. Well, one thing. I'll come back to that."

"Definitely the right place?"

"Yes. The police, of course, thought that I was an idiot who didn't know the difference between a dead man with a knife in his chest, and a dead sheep with nothing to show how it died. But while the police were there, I did a quick search and found a wheelbarrow track. Later, Eric and I went back to look. There was a wheelbarrow track from the lane almost to the spot. I looked more closely at the sheep. Definitely no sign of violence. So, we went to the sheep farmer a couple of miles away. Not a nice man. He said that he knew about the sheep, which must have wandered off."

"Well, you've been resourceful. But didn't the note make the police curious?"

"Er, no. I didn't tell them about the note because it went against the rules about not touching anything. I hadn't told them at the beginning because I assumed that they would see it when they looked at the body. After that, I don't why. Perhaps stubbornness. I was annoyed with them because they were being condescending and obtuse."

"And you want to solve the crime, don't you?"

Charity looked around innocently, then said, "Well, yes. And having not told them about the slip of paper, as with most lies and omissions, it's become worse with every passing minute. I suppose I should prepare for a reprimand and go and tell them. But it's just that ... they don't believe me about the body, so why would they believe me about a note on that body?"

The sound of a straw drawing powerfully in an empty glass made them aware of their full glasses. They drank, and Bernie insisted on buying the same again. "I don't buy many rounds," he said, "for the simple reason that I don't go in pubs, except for when I did what you did, which was to use the pub as a possible source of information. I have to be careful. My health. I'm prone to blackouts when I have stimulants, such as alcohol."

When he went to buy the drink, Charity said, "Well, assistant. Any thoughts so far?"

"I need more information."

"That's right. Did you enjoy the book?"

"It's not bad."

"Good. Keep reading it."

As she was talking, she was watching. A man who was leaving was accidentally impeded by someone entering. The man who was leaving tried to walk through the newcomer, but he was having none of it. As they walked round each other, she saw the face of the leaving man.

"That's the farmer," she said. "I didn't notice him earlier."

"He must have come in while you were talking. I was paying attention to what you were discussing."

"He wasn't in for long."

"Perhaps he was delivering some eggs."

"That his sheep had laid?"

"Perhaps he was delivering some wool."

When Bernie returned, she mentioned it. He said, "I was vaguely aware of someone at the bar when I was buying the drinks, and vaguely aware of his leaving. " He shrugged. "Well, farmers do drink in pubs."

She acknowledged this. After a sip of her drink, she said, "Bernie, I think that a further discharge of information from you is needed. You and Tom, your wife and Tom, the mystery Suzy."

"First, can you describe the dead man's waistcoat?"

"May," said Eric.

"No, Eric. He's asking me am I able to describe it. When I reply that I can, I am telling him that I *am* able to do it. May would be used ..."

"Er-hum."

"Yes. Sorry, Bernie. Later, Eric."

"No need."

"Yes, there is. But just at the moment, this is a higher priority. Go on, Bernie."

"*I'm* waiting for *you*."

"So you are. Oh, the waistcoat. It was green velvet, with gold edging on the pockets."

"Hmm. Anything else?"

"A lot of blood."

"I meant any other clothing?"

"Well, yes. He'd have looked very odd going around in a waistcoat and nothing else. Especially a green velvet one with gold edging."

After a polite pause, Bernie said, "No. I meant did you notice any of his other clothing?"

"Oh. Right. A tweedy sort of suit. The sort that I'd like. If I were a man. Possibly. In the winter."

"A cravate?"

"I don't think so. More of a large, red and yellow tie."

"Yes, he alternated. The tie was his informal dress."

"So was it your partner? Business one, I mean."

He sighed. "Certainly sounds like it."

"Any suspects, apart from your wife, Suzy, the farmer, and, keeping an open mind, you?"

"Oh, he had enemies. Business rivals, conservation groups, debtors, creditors, council members."

"Why councillors?"

"Councils, all councils, being corrupt, like to call the shots. They like things in addition to their personal and private payments. They like roundabouts, new flower beds, perhaps a children's playground or a skate park. Of course, the big guys, such as the supermarkets, have no problem with the big bribes, especially when any traffic improvements ease the traffic flow into their supermarkets. Tom wasn't in that league, and nowhere near it. He had no problem with making some payments, but he couldn't just hold out a wad and say, 'Go buy yourself a roundabout.' The council must be paid, the transport people must be paid, the police; architects and planners and designers, then all the people to build it and make all the changes to the roads."

"Surely they knew that."

"Yes. But that was just an example. Tom wanted to build some houses, but he wanted to build a leisure centre to attract people."

"Where did he want to build it?"

"On a couple of local fields."

"But wouldn't a leisure centre take care of a council's objections? Councils *like* leisure centres."

"They also like more money than Bernie was offering. You see, to satisfy council consciences about protecting the environment, you have to give them enough money to take away much more of the environment, and then you can give it impressive names about providing for the community, caring for your health, building much-needed housing, providing facilities for young people. Do enough of that and your village can soon become a newtown. Think of the increased power of a newtown council. And think of the money that has been received, collectively and individually."

"Is that what happened with your company?"

"Something of the sort. Certainly, it was a big failure for my marketing skills, such as they are. My marketing consists of persuasion through shared imagination, poster art, anything creative. I gave them the sweet stuff, then Tom gave them heartburn. All metaphorical, of course."

"Of course. Right up to his unmetaphorical murder."

"Or suicide," said the persistent one.

"Eric, be seen and not heard. And preferably not even seen."

Bernie chuckled. "Look, you have your hands full with your little nephew, and I'm not feeling my best. I have good days and bad days. Will you excuse me? We'll give it a couple of days and meet again. Here on Thursday, same time?"

"Yes, that's fine. Thank you for your help. But are you sure you're all right to drive?"

"Oh, yes. It isn't far. I just need to go home and close my eyes for a little while."

They shook hands. There was an awkward moment when Bernie offered a handshake to Eric, and the response was a raised hand for a 'high-five'. Bernie diplomatically touched hands, smiled at Charity and walked quickly away. The straight walk, the firm steps, reminded Charity of the concentrated walk of the secret drunk. She'd done it herself long ago. She started to think back to a memory of when she ...

"Eric! No!"

"It's not alcoholic," Eric said, putting Bernie's glass down. "Ew. Probably just as well. There's stuff at the bottom."

Charity snatched the glass, looked at the white crystals in the glass, and hurried out of the pub. She hurried across the car park and looked left and right.

She was just in time to see a car, swerve across the road, bounce off an approaching lorry and hit a tree.

CHAPTER TWELVE

"If you're not hungry," said Eric, "why don't we have takeaway?"

"For one thing, I can't be bothered to go and fetch it."

"No, silly. We can have it delivered."

"How decadent. And expensive. I've never done it. What do I do?"

"I'll do it. Give me your card, and tell me your PIN number."

"Pin. The *n* is for number. Saying number after it is … oh, never mind. Anyway, I don't like the idea of giving you my card and my PIN. You could buy the entire contents of a toy store."

"Toy store? Did mum tell you how old I am?"

"Yes. Well, I don't know what eleven year old monsters do these days. Play computer games? Send pointless messages to friends? Smoke pot? I've no idea. I'm not just out of touch, I've never been *in* touch."

"I'm a typical eleven year old boy."

"God help us."

"Well, anyway, I'm the only one here who knows how to order food to be delivered. Shall I do it?"

"Okay. I give in."

"Right. Let's see what there is round here. What do you like? Indian, Chinese or Italian?"

"Oh, you little man of the world. We're still talking about food, I presume. In which case, I don't mind."

"Okay. There isn't much choice within the usual distance. Italian seems the best bet. Pizza okay?"

"No takeaway spaghetti?"

"No. Pizza okay?"

"Looks like it."

"What sort?"

"Round and flat."

"What topping?"

"How topping. Er, cheese, tomato and mushrooms. With plenty of garlic. That does keep little boys away, doesn't it?"

"Hello? Yes, I'd like to order a takeaway, please."

She lay back and closed her eyes. The boy was in charge. Leave him to it. She let it flow over her, even the order for extra garlic bread and unnecessary drinks. Let it go, Charity. Today, there are more important things.

Such as an attempted murder to follow the actual one.

Somehow, Bernie had survived a brush with a lorry and a brutal encounter with a tree. It would be a while before she would be allowed to visit him. For one thing, his condition. Survival was one thing; returning to any sort of normality was very much a different matter.

And for another, she wasn't a relation.

On the other hand, she could loiter in the hospital and watch people who did visit, or at least tried to.

But before that, she had another plan.

"Eric," she said. "Would you like to do something naughty with me?"

"The pizzas will be here soon."

"Not now. Tomorrow."

"Er, yes, I suppose so."

"Good. I knew I could count on you. Eric, I'm going to break into the farmer's house."

"Oh. Won't that be dangerous?"

"Yes. Very. Your role will be very important."

"What's that?"

"You're going to open the gate and let the sheep out, and they might need some discreet encouraging."

"What if they stampede?"

"Do sheep stampede? Well, anyway, you'll be near the back, circling round them."

"Couldn't I just stand by the gate and call them?"

"No. For one thing, standing by the gate will make the sheep stand still, or hurry away from you; for another, I don't want any shouting. Discreet encouraging means creeping round the back and walking slowly towards them, persuading, speaking softly. I want the farmer to see the sheep when they have left the field, not in the middle of a one-boy rustle."

"A what?"

"Never mind. Concentrate. I'll go through it again tomorrow, but it's very simple. You open the gate, walk round the edge of the field, and coax the sheep down to the open gate."

"And you're counting on the farmer rushing out of his house and tearing after them."

"Yes. With his dogs. That's very important."

"What if he doesn't notice that his sheep have gone?"

"Well, I'm hoping that he's a vigilant sort of sheep farmer, constantly listening and watching."

"If he's constantly listening and watching, won't there be a big chance that he'll see me?"

"Ah, that will be the food," she said with relief as there was a pounding on the door.

It wasn't a long relief. In spite of various additional toppings, Eric still finished his pizza before Charity was half way through hers. After a satisfying, for him, burp, he resumed the discussion.

"So," he said, "what's the answer?"

"Eric, I am asking you to be naughty and sneaky and cunning. Is that something you don't want to do?"

"Well, if you put it like that."

She settled him down with the DVDs and the controller, and went over to her computer. Research, she told herself firmly. The first step in preparation.

It had occurred to her, much later than it should have done, that she was suspecting the farmer of foul deeds while continuing to call him the farmer. She needed more information. A quick search should at least provide a name. This wasn't sheep farming country. The internet did its best to confuse by widening the search to a radius of about thirty miles instead of just answering her question, but here he was. Roger McCarthy. Pretty plain. Nothing skulduggerous about that. Cotton Farm, The Coppice, Trench Lane, Hamingdon. No web site. He probably had something in the farmers' magazines, but nothing to provide any clues.

Facebook? So many. She became bored with that, and she was in danger of being distracted. One last try. And bingo! There he was. Profile photograph, a field of sheep. Topics, all about protecting the environment.

Especially my sheep fields?

Now for some distraction. She checked her emails. The history society was very keen to have her as a member, payment by direct debit. Oh, well, she reasoned, you mustn't expect to catch a murderer without a little expenditure. The next meeting of the local history group was tomorrow night. That would give Eric a little time to recover. She made the payment, using her card reader because the bankbot thought that the Hamingdon Local History Society might be an illegal organisation, and a £15 payment could cause financial problems for her.

She tapped in the village name and looked at the very varied results. There was one on the history of the place, and she had a look. No harm in being prepared for her first session. Not that there was much history. There was a lot of padding about the local soil and the probable trading and architectural habits of the Anglo-Saxons. Quite the busy and bustling place by the looks of it. Then the bullying Normans and the Angevins came with their rules and regulations, and they seemed to have done something bad to the weather. Bad crops, famine, plague, and lashings of religion. And plenty of lashings.

Nothing would ever convince her that Tostig's attack way up in the North of the Country, days before William's landing in the South East was a coincidence. Simple detective work, people. History likes to give people what they want: the easy version. Charity preferred to look at the facts and work things out for herself.

History. Not all long ago; some of it was recent. What was the recent history of Roger McCarthy and his sheep fields? He didn't seem to be a nice man, so were the sheep just a means of making a profit? Had he bought the farm, or inherited it?

She opened the old newspapers site. It wasn't cheap, but often the best way of studying history was through old newspapers, especially in the days, and newspapers, when news was simply reported, not accompanied by political opinions. But how recent would they be, and how much would there be for a village, near a small town, and a long way from a city?

She had to be shrewd with her searching. The nearest newspaper covered a wide area. The man's name was common, so was the word 'sheep'. She tried 'land', 'council' and 'disputes'. Plenty of niggling quarrels in the area covered by the newspaper, but nothing involving Mr McCarthy.

Until a small article from fifteen years ago. A firm called Bulstridge Developments had applied for planning permission to build forty houses on land at the Coppice, Hamingdon. Surprisingly, the application had been refused. No mention of Mr McCarthy, but it was useful information.

She began to yawn. Her forehead was almost touching the computer screen.

It was time for a little rest.

A little meditation.

She turned towards the loud sounds of fighting spaceships.

"What are you watching?"

"*Star Wars* of course?"

"Any good?"

"Course it is. What a stupid question."

She really needed some meditation.

How, with all this din?

She sat down next to Eric and said, "What's happened so far?"

CHAPTER THIRTEEN

B reakfast was finished, the blandest clothes had been selected , and Eric had been primed.

Charity was nervous. No, more than nervous.

"Let fear be my motivator!" she cried, as though Eric were an army.

"You just have to slip into the house when it's all clear," Eric grumbled. "I'm the one who has to organise these sheep out of a field, possibly while being watched by an angry farmer, who probably deals with rustlers by firing at them with a shotgun."

"I'm sorry, Eric. If I'd known that you were a trembling wimp, I'd not have asked."

"I'm not a wimp, and I'm not afraid of doing it. I was just pointing out my danger."

"I do understand, Eric, and I appreciate your bravery. We're both afraid, and we need our different motivators. Mine is the challenge of fear. Yours is proving that you're not a wimp."

With the brief mutiny quelled, it was time to go and accept the challenge. It was time to …

There was a loud knock at the door. Charity looked at Eric. He shrugged. "No use looking at me."

She opened the door, and there was, here was, one of the biggest disappointments of her entire life. There was never a right time for Uncle Ken, but this was a particularly bad time.

But what could she do?

"Uncle Ken. What a lovely surprise," she warbled stoically.

"Were you going out?"

"Just for a walk."

"Well, I shan't stay long. I was going this way, and I thought I'd call in. Have you decided about the garden yet?"

"No. It's a difficult one."

"Noo, it's not difficult. I did all the thinking for you. You just have to give me the go-ahead, and I'll do it all for you."

He paused very briefly. "Like my tattoos, do you?" he said to Eric. "The swallow and the anchor. Two popular navy tattoos."

"Were you in the navy?"

"Could have been, should have been. Eyesight not good enough. Broke my heart. And my father's."

"Couldn't you see the enemy ships, like Nelson?"

"Oh, I could see well enough, just not, well, well enough."

He let out what Charity called his sad salute sigh and shook his head. "Had all the skills. Just not the eyesight."

He clapped his hands. "Still, no good moping. I've used

my skills in lots of other ways. So, what do you think? Shall I make a start? I have all my power tools in the car."

He loooked down at Eric. "I don't go far without my tools. I have all anyone could need. Power drills, power washers, power screwdrivers. Power's what you need to do a good job."

Back to Charity. "So, yes to the pond? I'll design it for you. Lilies, flags, put in some koi and goldfish."

"Won't the koi attack the goldfish?"

"Well, you'd have to check up on that. I'm just making suggestions. And I could rig you up a fountain, connect it to the water supply. I could fix up some lighting. Really impress the neighbours."

"I don't want to impress the neighbours."

"I can see that."

"Well, let me have a think."

"That's what you said last time."

"It's a big step, a lot of money, and a lot of disruption."

"Well, whatever you decide to do with it, and it's just a mess as it is, needs something doing to it, let me know. Don't go buying stuff. You don't know what to buy. And don't pay anyone to do it. I'm your man."

"Thank you. I do appreciate it. And I do like ponds. But I really should have a vegetable garden."

"You could have that, too."

"I mean the whole garden."

"*Vege*tables. That's why you have shops. Your garden's your social centre. It's your ... statement of who you are. Lawn, pond, barbecue."

"I expect you could build a barbecue."

"No problem."

Charity winced to indicate thought, doubt and probable

submission. "Okay. I'll do something, very soon, and I'll call you in straightaway."

"Do that. And soon. I always have a lot on. People with my skills are in demand."

"I know. Thanks for thinking of me. I'll decide on something very soon. I promise."

"When the door was closed, Eric said, "What a big bag of ...."

"Thank you, Eric. Yes, he's one of life's great know-alls. And I always say that the biggest problem with know-alls is that they don't. If I have a pond and it leaks, or a barbecue and it collapses, Uncle Ken will sniff and say, 'You can't buy decent materials these days. Everything's poor quality. Never mind. I'll sort out the mess. This is where the *real* skill comes in.'"

She grinned as Eric laughed. "However," she said, "the silly old sod has shown me what to do next."

"In the garden?"

"No. At the farm."

By crouching down by the gate, they were out of sight of anyone in the farm house. Charity did a quick inspection and said, "Surprisingly, it's exactly as I hoped it would be. One wooden gate on the verge of collapse, one ditto gatepost, and one fence supported by brambles."

She looked sternly at Eric. "Well, assistant. Do you think you can do this?"

He studied the rotten wood with the air of an expert and nodded. "Oh, I think I can manage that."

"Good. Remember: everything must be pulled out this

way, as though the sheep had leaned against the wood or run into it."

"Yup. Understood."

"And let them see the carrots, without looking sinister.

He looked blank. They both let that one pass.

"Right. I'll meet you back at the oak tree. Dead Body Point."

He liked that new name for it. Anything to keep him interested.

With a bent back, Charity scuttled along the bushes, trying not to hear the cracking and crunching behind her. Eric wasn't trying the subtle approach; he was tearing the gate to pieces. It was going to look as though the sheep had all gone mad together and hacked their way out.

When she reached the lane, the brambles became a hedge, and she made a right-angled turn towards the farm house. She paused and peered through the brambles into the field. The sheep weren't showing any interest in the carrot treat being offered. Perhaps the original plan would have been better.

Carried on the breeze, Eric's voice was clear and sharp. "Come on, you stupid sheep. What's the matter with you?"

She was about to mutter, when she heard the rough sound of a vehicle. It suggested the ubiquitous farm Discovery chugging towards her. She combined a crawl into the brambles with a curl into a ball. The vehicle went past. A glance showed that it was what she had guessed. Mr McCarthy was leaving. She hoped that he was keeping his eyes on the road and hadn't seen her in the hedge or Eric off to the right, crouched by a shattered gate with a supply of carrots, possibly being approached by a lot of sheep.

This wasn't necessarily a better version. She'd wanted

him to rush out of the house and down the fields, not thinking about locking his doors, and taking his dogs. Going out to drive somewhere, he probably had locked up, and left his dogs in the house. She'd brought some doggy treats, just in case, but doubling as guard dogs, they might prefer some human flesh. Oh, well. She wouldn't find out by crouching in a hedge, and she didn't know when he'd be back. She uncoiled and hurried along the lane, glad that the house was isolated, well away from prying eyes.

The front door was locked. The dogs announced their intention of tearing her to bits if she touched the house again. She went round to the back, determined to try before hurrying away. With a clank, the handle turned and she pushed the door open.

The dogs hurtled in. Four very protective collies.

Charity leaned forward and spread her arms. "Hello, lovely doggies," she said in her best welcome voice. "*Good* doggies. *Lovely* doggies." With slow, gentle movements, she put out her arms, giving them the choice of tearing her to bits or having some fondling.

Showing her confidence and submission, she knelt as she fondled, putting her face close, inviting kisses.

"Oh," she said as they wriggled and squirmed around her. "You really *are* lovely doggies. You need lots of love and affection, don't you? And lots of *this*." She scratched all their heads and jiggled their ears.

What was the next step? The dogs might be very happy to have her company in the kitchen, giving her the benefit of the doubt and all that, but they might think that exploring the house was overdoing it. *Come on, now. We let you in the kitchen, but going upstairs is really too much. Oh,*

*not the bedroom! No, we must stop you there. Please! Don't
make us do this.*

She passed out some treats, and walked softly away.

She suddenly saw a vast gulf between her amateur
dabblings and real detective work. She had no plan. She had
a vague notion of walking in and seeing bloodstained
clothes soaking in a bucket in the kitchen, and incriminating documents on the table in the lounge.

She went quickly into the long main room, which
seemed to be a combined hall, lounge, sitting room and
dining room, beneath attractive low beams. No visible
documents. A couple of agriculture magazines, yesterday's
newspaper.

She wanted to leave. This wasn't worth the risk.

A quick look upstairs. Then at least she could tell herself
that she had done her best and examined the whole house.

The staircase was wide, not carpeted, well-polished oak.
She was almost purring. What a beautiful house. Much too
good for McCarthy.

"Concentrate!" she snapped at herself. "Concentrate on
the job."

Hurrying along the wide landing, she checked the rooms.
Bathroom, box room, small empty bedroom, master bedroom.
She hesitated. Suddenly, investigating had deteriorated into
prying, snooping. She was very strict about her own privacy;
now it seemed hypocritical. If she had strong evidence of his
guilt, it might be different. As it was …were those real leaded
light windows. Yes, they were. How wonderful to start each day
by looking out at the beautiful, gently undulating countryside.

How terrible to see the Discovery below her.

When did he arrive? How long did she have?

The only way out was downstairs, which might mean running down as he entered the house.

She heard the front door open.

The dogs came out with formal politeness, no doggy enthusiasm, until they saw Charity on the stairs. They whimpered.

She was trapped.

"Hey, mister," called a familiar voice. "Your sheep are out of the field. I just saw them."

"Why were you anywhere near my sheep?"

"Out walking. Nothing wrong with that is there?"

"That depends."

"Depends on what?"

She realised that Eric was stalling, trying to give her time. Trying to be fast, but silent, she crept down several steps. She could see the front door, slightly open.

The dogs were gathering round her, almost begging.

In the next moment, McCarthy might lose patience with the boy, and he might wonder about the dogs.

With a follow-me gesture, she dashed stealthily down the last few steps, over the wooden floor, into the kitchen. In a ludicrous pause, she cuddled all the dogs, then gave them the treats. She gripped the handle of the back door, then hesitated. With the front door open, opening this door might cause a draught. She went back and eased the inner door closed. She could hear the irritated voice of McCarthy and the persistent voice of Eric.

The next obstacle was the clanky handle. She held the latch as she turned the handle. A bit of a squeak. That would do. She squeezed out and stopped again.

Where to go?

She started to go round the side of the house. She might be able to listen to the discussion.

But the discussion had stopped.

She'd made the wrong choice. Heavy footsteps and angry muttering were about to come round the corner.

She swung round, and leapt behind a concrete coal bunker.

A moment later, the heavy footsteps and the muttering were very loud.

"Interfering little brat. Damn nuisance sheep. The sooner those damn houses are built, the better."

The back door was opened, and he called, "Here! Out, out, out. Go and round up those damn sheep."

Don't come to me! Don't come to me!

Deep relief as the dogs followed Nasty McCarthy's command and rushed off across the yard towards the fields. They were followed by the clumping human. She crawled out from her hiding place, ran round to the front of the house and into the lane.

CHAPTER FOURTEEN

"Are you clear about everything?"

One of Eric's rewards was being left for a couple of hours while Charity went to the Local History group. He was set up like an invalid on the armchair, supplied with DVDs, the book, which he occasionally read, crisps, sweets, cans of fizzy stuff, and, most important, his mobile telephone, with Charity's number in it.

"Yes."

"Remember, if you catch fire, don't rush out into the street. Roll around until the flames go out."

"How could I catch fire? There isn't a fire, and I'm not going to cook anything."

"The television might explode. Your telephone might overheat. Wiring might catch fire."

"Let's just assume that nothing freaky is going to happen in the next two hours, but if it does, I'll ring you, then call 999 and tell them there's a fire."

"Don't answer the door to *anyone*."

"Not even the fire people?"

"That's a separate worry. This is the murdering, molesting abductors."

"Murdering, then molesting? Ew."

"Vile people who do vile things."

Eric looked pointedly at the window. "In Hamingdon?"

"It's important to prepare for the unlikely things. I shall lock you in."

"But what if there's a fire, not on me, and I need to run out?"

"I shall put the spare key ... on the bookcase. Use only if there's an emergency. Not for any visitors."

"Have you locked the back door?"

She pointed at him. "Good point."

When she came back, Eric said, "Please go, Charity. You'll make me nervous if you keep on. And you promised me a relaxing evening. You can trust me. You've seen how well I can do."

"I have indeed, and you know how impressed I was. But there's always the danger that you'll sink back into ..."

"What?"

"Well, vacant adolescence. Television, iPad, crisps, pop ..."

"*Pop?* People stopped calling it pop in the middle ages."

"They didn't have fizzy drinks in the middle ages. Well, apart from fermenting beer and wine."

"Well, you know what I mean."

"People wouldn't have to say 'Well, you know what I mean' if they didn't say something obtuse or confusing. You mean that a few years ago, perhaps twenty or thirty, people stopped saying 'pop'."

"Yes. You're a pretty old-fashioned person."

"I like to think that I'm not so much *old*-fashioned as *non*-fashioned."

"You're going to be late for your meeting."

"Gosh, you're right."

"And people don't say 'gosh' anymore." He laughed. "You really do belong in an old film."

"A silent comedy or a thriller?"

"Definitely a silent comedy. Constantly tripping over things and falling in puddles."

"Hardly a female role in an old film."

"Well…"

"I'm going to be late."

He nodded firmly. Some things are better left unsaid.

A quick sprint, without tripping over anything, and she wasn't late. But pulling the push door, lurching in with a touch of dishevelment, and feeling moisture in her armpits, wasn't the best start. Then, she had the new recruit embarrassment of being introduced to everyone, and, the horror for which she should have prepared, being asked what her local history interests were. She waffled. She began with, "This might seem to be a small, insignificant village, but there is important history in the smallest acts…." and took it from there.

She stopped when she saw the eyes starting to glaze, which didn't take long. There were murmurs of agreement and approval, and the secretary said, "We all agree." He didn't refer to any specific bit in her short oratory, but it was comforting. She tried to put murder and eleven year old boys out of her mind and settled back to learn.

It was interesting, but she had to concentrate because the topics veered about, a few centuries this way, a few centuries that; and there were frequent references to 'the

war'. Every period had 'the war'. Hamingdon's major role
in all these wars seemed to consist of being in the way or
on the way. Armies that wanted to fight where
Hamingdon was inconveniently standing had to go off and
find a large field in which to do it. After a battle, the
winning side would maraud like a lot of football hooli-
gans, leaving the village short of alcohol, food and young
women. On the other hand, when an army was passing
through on its way to a battle, it would forgo the
marauding and just take the alcohol, food and young
women.

She reminded herself that this was just the very slow
means to an end. It wasn't going to be a long series of
historical events leading to the dead body in the wood. She
settled down and did her best to retain the information.

When it was over, there was an informal gathering for
tea and biscuits. Time for some gentle interrogation. She
floated about, catching eyes, all but dragging people into
conversation.

"What did you think of it?" asked a small, rosy-cheeked
man, exuding hay and history.

"Very interesting," Charity replied. "Very stimulating."

"We haven't been called that before, have we Len?" said
an approaching tall and muscular woman, who looked as
though she wasn't Len's wife.

"Certainly haven't. Most people think we're a lot of old
bores."

Charity smiled. "Well, most people are usually wrong."

"True. I'm Len Brent, this is Alison Chudleigh. You
probably instantly forgot everyone's name."

"It's a defect of mine, Bill."

He laughed politely. She hurried on, leaving the feeble

joke behind. "Have you been studying the local history for a long time?"

"Oh, how long have we been doing this, Ally? Twenty two years?"

"Yes, about that. But local history as a subject is only part of what we do. We take a keen interest in the connected topics of preservation and conservation." She looked round. "Which reminds me. No Roger tonight."

"Oh, yes," Len said, mildly puzzled.

Another man leaned in. "Probably still mending his gate and fence. His sheep burst through and scattered. Took him a while to bring them all in."

"Ah, we'll let him off, then." He turned to Charity. "Roger McCarthy. Our keenest member. Our real farmer. Not many of them left. Mostly big industrialised combines now."

"On the little bit of land that hasn't been built on," added the new man.

"This is Lorne," Len said.

"Unfortunately, I don't have one. Rockeries, shrub-beries, vegetables and herbs, but no lawn."

The little group chuckled politely.

Well, Charity thought, the door has been opened. Let's go through it.

"Has Mr McCarthy been here for a long time?"

Len answered. "His father was. He died a couple of years ago, and his son came to take over."

"Was his son already a sheep farmer?"

"Done all sorts. Been all over."

"But not involved with his father's farm?"

"No. His father worked mostly alone. Sheep are low maintenance, they tell me. He had occasional help. We used to call one the old shepherd. He died. And there was Granger. Lorne, what happened to Granger?"

"Died."

Charity mentally tutted. All these potential witnesses dying. It wasn't good enough. She decided to push on. "It's good to see a real working farm these days. Most villages are being ruined by housing estates and factories."

"It certainly is," agreed Alison. "There is constant pressure on farmers to sell, but Roger is adamant that he won't be tempted. And we're very grateful that he has joined our society. In a short time, he has become one of our stalwarts."

Nodding vigorously, Len said, "Helped us with our opposition to the application to build forty houses on Dean's Meadow. We won that one."

Charity was giving the appropriate facial indications of approval and admiration, with enthusiastic little 'hmms'.

"Can we count on your support with any petitions and campaigning?" Alison asked.

"Yes. Definitely," she replied, wondering what would happen when an application to build on Mr McCarthy's land appeared.

She hadn't found any documents or murder evidence at the farm, but she had heard very clearly what Mr McCarthy's intentions were.

CHAPTER FIFTEEN

Charity was given permission to visit Bernie. He looked pale and very tired, and very bruised and cut, but he rallied when he saw her.

"I'm under police investigation. The doctors have confirmed that there are faint traces of something unpronounceable, for me, in my system, which they say in their usual way could have a variety of sources."

"I suspect the traces were faint because some of the stuff stayed in your glass. I ran out to warn you. Why didn't you do that middle-aged man thing of sitting for a while, adjusting your position, struggling with the seat belt, adjusting your mirror, looking around in case a woman with a pram had walked behind you."

He looked down. "Don't tell the police, Charity. It's that old joke."

She thought for a moment, then slapped her forehead. "Ah. You decided to hurry home before you had a blackout."

"Silly, wasn't it?"

"Very. Especially when you were right by a reviving pub, where you could flush the stuff out with mineral water, and where I and my little helper would have been willing to help you."

"You're making me feel terrible."

"So you should. You could have hit a woman with a pram. As it was, you deservedly hit a tree instead. The tree survived, by the way."

While Bernie did the Nod of Shame, she began to tell him of her progress. He listened patiently, but when she finished, he said, "Charity, I think you've lost your right to reprimand me for being stupid."

"No. Let's reprimand each other. None of that wiping the slate clean. Your folly is still on our private record."

"Next to yours."

"Next to mine. Although mine did have a worthwhile purpose, and outcome."

"I accept that. Now, what are we to do with the bits of knowledge?"

As she started to think, another thought barged in. "Bernie, while you're in here, and Tom is dead somewhere, who is running the business?"

"That is a very good question. No-one is officially running it as such. The staff are keeping it from collapse. But one particular member of staff is probably running it. Or thinking she is. Marie Ridings. She used to give orders to Tom. I was out of it most of the time, popping in and out, but I saw and heard things. You probably know the type. Because people above them in rank become dependent on them, they assume command. Tom and I did what was necessary and left her to run the rest of the staff, all twelve of them."

"How did you explain Tom's absence?"

"A bereavement. Someone who was very dear to him."

"A neat avoidance of a lie."

"I thought so."

"Are the staff loyal?"

He mused. "Loyal staff. Do they even exist nowadays?"

"That's a depressing thought."

"When you're running a business, you have to live with the depressing thoughts."

"Well, here's another one. While you're in here, all those individuals might come together to form a unit containing twelve members, with this Ridings person in charge. Confidential information might be shared. Passwords. Documents. Things that you wouldn't want the staff to see. Things which *I* might want to see."

They looked at each other. Bernie said, "In the present difficult circumstances, I think that a temporary office manager is needed. When can you start?"

"Office junior?" Eric protested. "I'm too young to be left on my own all day, but I'm old enough to work in an office?"

"Not work, Eric. There are laws against that. And your parents. No, this would be merely ... fetching and carrying, emptying things, photocopying, perhaps making the tea."

"So, office drudge."

"Not very long ago, that's how most young people started their working lives. And for many, not much had changed by the time they retired."

"Will they pay me?"

"*I'll* pay you, unofficially. And keep reminding yourself

that this has a purpose. No naughtiness. No mischief. No smart alec quips. I need to be accepted as a temporary office manager, appointed by the boss.I shall be Caroline Holt. I'm going to put on an act. So must you."

"Act as what?"

"An office drudge. A willing one. An enthusiastic one. Just for a few days. To help me. To help Bernie. To help the investigation."

She combined pitiful plea with winsome wile. Eric sank into deep thought. Deep for him, that is.

"How much are you going to pay me?"

"It will be performance-related pay, Eric. Do a good job for me, and I shall be generous, even though, as my assistant, I expect you to put the job first at all times."

"What if I do a bad job?"

"No pay, and marmalade with shreds."

"That's pretty brutal."

"I'm investigating a murder, an attempted murder, and a lot of skulduggery, and you're calling *me* brutal?"

Sidestepping, he said, "So what are *you* going to be doing while I'm toiling away?"

She sighed and shrugged. "I don't really know. Partly, I'm there to keep the staff working, partly to do some sort of work by ensuring that things go out, and that things that come in are dealt with, and partly to snoop. I'm going to be looking for evidence, perhaps a blackmail note, anything that might have led to this man's death. Bernie knows the email address and personal password for this Tom, so I can, yes can, look on the computer for any emails to do with this. Hmm."

"Hmm?"

"Just a thought. I think that it isn't only the message on

that slip of paper that's important. The fact that his message was on a slip of paper is significant."

"How do you mean?"

"Thirty years ago, and many years before that, a boy of your age would have been confronted with two horrors after Christmas. One, going back to school; two, writing at least one thank you letter to an old relation. Now, imagine that it's next Christmas. Having proved my usefulness, and hopefully earned the gratitude of your parents, and you, I might buy a present for you. Now, a nice boy like you wouldn't display a lack of gratitude. What would you do?"

"Send you a message."

"Perhaps you know that I'm old-fashioned …"

"I do know."

"And perhaps you know that I *like* to receive a letter in the old-fashioned way. What would you do?"

"Send a message."

She looked him with encouragingly raised eyebrows.

"Oh, I see. Ah, right. The woman, Suzy, sent him a written note instead of a text message or an email."

"Exactly. Which suggests two things. No, three things. Not necessarily all of them. One, the sender of the message didn't want to trust leaving evidence on a computer. Two computers. Or whatever. Two, the sender of the message didn't have access to the email account of the person from whom the message was supposed to have come. Three, that the sender of the message was close enough to be able to pass a written message."

She looked at him. "Well?"

"I'm thinking."

"Oh." She didn't want to disturb this unexpected occurrence.

Eric raised a finger and said, "You need to find this Suzy."

She beamed. "Good boy, Eric. You hit the nail on the head. Either she wrote the note or she didn't write the note. If she did, then we might have found the murderer or the accomplice. The setter-up. The enticer. If she didn't, then the murderer knew about whatever relationship she had with Tom and knew that he would come to her."

"And the murderer must have known that Tom knew which great oak, and if it was Suzy, then she knew that Tom knew which great oak, but if it was the murderer, he must have known that Tom and Suzy both knew which great oak, unless … what was I saying?"

"You've covered the main points. Impressive. With you as my assistant, I am confident of success."

Eric grinned. "With me as your assistant, so am I."

CHAPTER SIXTEEN

"What do you think?"

Eric looked at her with sarcastic appraisal, and said, "Do you need to be tarted up for an office?"

"I am not tarted up. I am dressed … in my best. I need to convince a lot of people that I'm a consultant with long experience and expertise in the building industry, with a knowledge of financial systems and computer programmes, and with managerial experience."

"No wonder you're tarted up. It's your only hope."

"And *your* bit of acting is to convince the same people that you are a decent, conscientious office junior. Think you can manage that?"

"Hmm. It's a lot to ask."

"And if you don't co-operate, the money that you need for the purchase of your eagerly anticipated DVD will be a lot to ask."

"This is blackmail."

"No, it isn't. It's called incentivisation."

"Same thing."

"Well, to the extent that it is, which it isn't, you'll find a lot of other things in life which are the same thing, depending on how you look at them, positively or negatively. For example, detention. Is it a punishment or an incentivisation? Or both?"

"When Miss Jenkins does it, it's purely punishment."

"That *might* be how she looks at it. But that isn't important. What *is* important is how *you* look at it. Whatever it was that annoyed her, you can decide not to do it again. And with a small step towards wisdom, you could anticipate and avoid other things that might annoy her."

"There's a lot of things that annoy her."

"That increases the challenge."

She picked up a bulging old briefcase. "The final touch. The bulging briefcase of the busy office worker."

"What's in it?"

"Some of my heaviest books."

She looked at her watch. "Time to go. And my first challenge is to find this place while driving through heavy traffic. I'm not looking forward to it. However, it must be done. It's a grim means to a very worthwhile end."

Fortunately, for Charity, the office was on an industrial estate on the outskirts of the town. Having seen it on her right, she went round the next roundabout and drove back. There wasn't a car park as such, just a parking area with already-fading parking space markings. And there was no space available. She switched to her new role and parked anywhere, blocking at least four cars.

"It's up to them to provide a parking space for me," she said. Seeing doubt on Eric's face, she added, "Yes, I know

I'm a fake appointment by the boss, but they don't know that. I mean the fake bit. I'm *his* appointment, and it's up to them to co-operate with me."

"Go, girl," said Eric with mock enthusiasm. "You show them who's boss."

She put her head back and said, "You're right. Diplomacy. Firm, but polite. Strong, but considerate. But I'm still leaving my car here, mainly on the grounds that I don't know where else I can, may, park. "

Before they were allowed in, they were required to speak into a tin box beside the door. The crackly voice said, "I don't have a boy on the approval sheet."

"I had hoped that Bernie would mention it. My current domestic circumstances leave me no choice but to bring my son with me. Usually, I work from home, but I have answered this emergency call from Bernie, and I expect co-operation for the short period of my assistance. Moreover, my son, familiar with procedure through helping me at home, can be useful here."

"That wouldn't be permitted. Health and Safety, insurance, employment of minors."

Eric whispered, "Stay calm."

She took a deep breath and said, "Just a moment. I'll call Bernie."

Considering that he was still thickly bandaged, in the depths of a hospital, Bernie soon answered, and she told him the problem.

Bernie said, "I should have realised you'd take the boy with you. They're annoyingly right. I'll speak to them. Be patient. Try not to rub them up the wrong way."

A few minutes later, the door slid open, and they

walked through to the reception desk. The young man said, "Sorry about this, but we have to follow all the rules. Mr Pocket suggested that your son sit in the store room. We'll show him where the toilets are and the water dispenser, and he can be supplied with cans from the dispenser, cups of tea if he wants."

"Okay. Not satisfactory, but if that's what the rules say, there's nothing we can do about it. Is someone going to show us where things are?"

"Of course. Ms Ridings, the Head of Admin, is on her way down. Ah, here she is now."

A door opened and a very smartly-dressed woman approached them, already gushing bonhomie. Charity whispered, "All these young people are making me feel old."

"Miss Holt! Welcome to PH Developments. This is a very interesting time for us, two bosses down, so to speak, but we're coping well, as always. I understand that you've come to help us to cope. I'll take you to Mr Pocket's office."

"Thank you," Charity said, following her through the door. As they went up some clanky, vibrating steps, she resumed the conversation. "Yes. But not to cut across your established ways of efficiency, not to ruffle feathers. At Mr Pocket's level, there are professional links, such as my consultancy services, which are useful in different ways throughout Industry. Technical, legal, in all its forms, design, environmental. The list is almost endless. So are the levels of consultancy and managerial service provision. In this case, owing to the unusual circumstances, it was thought that an actual presence might be beneficial."

"Of course," Miss Ridings said with icy sweetness as they reached a landing. She indicated the toilets and a vending machine. They went through another door and along a narrow corridor.

"However," Charity continued, "I must emphasise that my purpose is to assist, not to interfere. All those things that are working well may continue to work well. If a problem should arise, and not be resolved, then I, or Mr Pocket, would attend to it. I have plenty of knowledge and experience, but I have my limitations where the day-to-day running of a business is concerned."

"That's good," Miss Ridings said, lowering the temperature by a few more degrees. "Here is the office. It isn't very big, but we have very little space, and Mr Pocket is very down-to-earth."

It certainly wasn't very big. It wasn't any sort of big. A desk, with a metal frame and stick-on wood effect, with a computer on top, a couple of chairs, three metal filing cabinets, and one window.

"Commendably so," Charity said. "Is Mr Henry's office the same as this one?"

"Slightly bigger, and he has an old wooden desk which he brought with him."

Charity had a brief mental picture of a joint partner arriving bent over with a wooden desk on his back. But she kept that to herself.

As she struggled to make some approving noises in her throat, a penetrating voice said, "What the *hell's* my room going to be like?"

That didn't take long. Eric's brief career in diplomacy had lasted all of five minutes.

Miss Riding's look suggested that she hadn't previously been aware of him, but now she was, she didn't like what she heard and saw. "You will have adequate space for someone who is not an employee or … a temporary office manager.

Having received a laser look from Charity, Eric clammed up and nodded like Noddy.

Miss Ridings led them up a narrow staircase to a room which was large, but almost filled with cabinets, cupboards, old computers, and other items of discarded office furniture. There was a small skylight in the ceiling, but no window.

Charity said, "So this is where items of old office furniture come to die."

"Something like that. Well, young man. There are plenty of chairs here. Most are merely obsolete, and should be safe to sit on, though I do advise a quick test first. Someone will be up with a drink shortly. Miss Shields and I need to run through a few essential things."

"Okay, Eric?" Charity said affectionately. "Make yourself as comfortable as you can, and I'll pop in now and then."

"Oh, I'll be fine," he replied stoically.

"Good," said Miss Ridings, drawing a firm line under the problem of the boy.

For the next hour or so, with brisk clarity, Miss Ridings explained the computer system, the administration system, the finance system, the national and international regulations, conservation, and the customer database. The longer that it went on, the fuzzier it became. Charity just kept saying, "Ah, yes," and "Right," as though it were all familiar or all made sense.

"Normally," the guide said, "you'd have a couple of weeks at least of training and gradual induction, but being thoroughly experienced, it's really just a matter of showing you where things are. Can you think of anything I've missed?"

"Mr Pocket explained that the company system password changes automatically every three days. I'll need to know it."

"Well, the system here is that when someone without security clearance uses the computer system, I do the start-up and log in so it's all ready for you when you come in. I start early."

Charity took her time, letting her opponent know that she was searching for the right words. "Miss Ridings, please understand that I am here at the express wish of the joint owner of this company, to perform certain special functions, for the purpose of ensuring that the customary efficiency is maintained in his absence. In order to do that I need, and have Mr Pocket's full permission to have, access to all aspects of the business, including, of course, the computer system."

"And that's why I'll…"

Charity raised a hand. "No! First, because of what I have just explained. Second, what would happen if you were knocked down, or otherwise prevented from appearing at your usual time?"

"One of the other people…"

"One of the people whom I have come to supervise would come and put in the password for me? I do not work that way. I'm trying to be diplomatic, but I won't have obstacles put in the way of my job performance. Now, I don't want to bother Mr Pocket again when he is recovering from his accident, so I'll leave the choice to you."

"Very well. I shall place on record that I stated my objection and was, presumably, overrruled."

"Not presumably. I'll put it bluntly, which I had been trying so hard to avoid. *I* am in charge in Mr Pocket's absence. When he returns, or makes a different arrangement, I shall depart. Until then, let's work together to keep this company running well."

"Yes," was the reply, so distant that it seemed to come from the next county. "I'll write it down."

Charity found a notepad in the desk and Miss Ridings wrote the password.

"Thank you," Charity said pleasantly. "Right. I'll play around with this, and it probably won't be long before I need assistance. I don't want to keep bothering you. Is there a general help person in the place?"

"That would be Linda Coles. She's moved around a lot internally, so she has a good general knowledge of how everything works. Her extension is 646."

"Perfect. Thank you... I do hope it isn't part of the system that we address one another by surnames."

"No, except on formal occasions, such as visitors or speaking to the bosses, we use first names."

Charity looked at her, patiently waiting for a response.

"Oh. Marie."

"And I'm Caroline. Thank you, Marie."

Marie didn't look at her ease after being stripped of her robe of formality, but she managed a little smile before she left. Charity turned on the computer, tapped in the password and waited while the big fluid silver blobs coiled and swirled around and through the logo of the system provider. Then came the warnings, cookie choices, undertakings, invitations to upgrade and renew. When that was done, a sort of menu appeared in the form of pictures. After a few mistakes, she called up email and entered Tom Henry's email address and password.

There were a lot of emails, and a lot of folders.

Surely in all this, there was bound to be at least one small clue.

CHAPTER SEVENTEEN

Marie hadn't closed the door when she left. Charity heard the tap and saw her visitor simultaneously.

"Terry Stance," he said. "Chief Negotiator, amongst other things."

"Pleased to meet you. Have you come to negotiate with *me*?"

"Oh, no," he laughed. "A little advice, if it's convenient."

Uh-oh.

"I'll do my best. Have a seat. What's the problem?"

"Well, what do you know about KLZ?"

Charity held up a hand, politely. "Mr Stance, when people want me to do something for them, they usually ask me what I'll be doing on the appropriate date; and I always tell them to tell me what they want me to do. Let's skip the introductory questions and go straight to the matter on which you want my advice."

A sensible approach which neatly covered up her ignorance about KLZ. The return of serve caused some confusion, which suggested that he was working from a script.

"Oh. Right. Um, well, KLZ is our biggest supplier of foundation materials. Concrete, wood, stone, and so on, depending on what we're building and where."

"And for what cost?"

"Er, yes, although we always ensure that whatever materials are used, the foundation is entirely adequate for the building which will stand on it."

"Of course. Carry on."

"Well, KLZ operate as most contractors do, by putting in their tender with all sorts of things to increase their profits. Actual profit is just part of it. There are overheads and contingencies. It's all a big fiddle, of course, as I'm sure you know. They open up the factory in the morning, and turn on the lights, then charge for lighting on every contract. The person who empties the bins turns up on every contract. As for contingencies, they and we identify the risks, they charge for the potential risk, and then when something happens, they ask for more money to put it right."

Charity nodded knowledgeably. "Paid twice," she said. "Once for the thing that might happen, twice when the thing does happen."

"Exactly."

"And that happens at every stage, with all the subcontractors, I presume."

"Yes."

"Do you have any government, council contracts?"

"Some."

"And partly to recoup your costs, you do the same?"

He shrugged theatrically. "*Have* to, otherwise we'd go under."

"Okay. Well, so far we've just gone over familiar ground. What's the problem with … KLZ?"

"They are doing the contingency fiddle in a big way. We can't afford what they are demanding."

"Even if we could, we'd be very foolish to pay it."

"They are the only reliable supplier, their prices aren't bad, even allowing for the fiddling, and we don't have the time to go anywhere else."

"And they know it."

"Yes."

Charity thought back to one of her early jobs, when she learned a lot simply by listening. One sour old man used to treat every problem with the same response: *What does it say in the contract?*

When people talked about necessities and practicalities, he would shake his head, becoming irritated and say that the first step must always be to look at the contract. People didn't like his dogmatic obstinacy, but even though her job had been only a few levels above Eric's intended job, she had understood what he was saying.

"Terry," she said slowly. "Was the thing that has gone wrong included in the list of identified risks?"

"Yes."

"Was that list part of the contract?"

"Yes. One of the annexes."

"And their prices, including contingency, are part of the contract?"

"Yes."

"Then that is your negotiating starting point."

"Pointing at the contract doesn't work in the real world."

"What happens in the real world is that everyone assumes that losses can be passed on and compensated for by the next person in the chain. They say that it can't be done for that price. Let's say that you're building something for the council…"

"Which we are."

"So you'll expect the council to disregard your contract with them, and pay you what you demand."

"Yes."

"And then the council will ask *you*, Terry Stance, for more money through your council tax. And everyone in the chain thinks that it all worked out very well, and so long as everyone plays ball, it can go on working well. Terry, it needs someone to say, 'No'. You say 'No', and tell them to tell their subcontractor 'No'.

"But if the little outfit right at the start of the chain insists that it's going to put them out of business…"

"It's a modern disease: pass the problem on and let someone else sort it out. The cost of something goes up, so a company puts the price up, instead of first thinking for a way of dealing with the problem. And it goes all the way up the chain. A price goes up, so the next price goes up. And at the end of the chain is the buyer, who has to pay for a long chain of price rises."

"Well, what do you suggest?"

"Negotiate! You have your contract for a starting point. No deviation from the contract. Breach of contract means big trouble. Next, you look for points of compromise. How can we reduce costs without reducing quality? What if *we* do this and *you* do that? Flexibility. Innovation. There are always different ways of doing things. But most important is that *they* must do this with *their* sub-contractors, all the way back down the chain."

He nodded with the determination of a clump of seaweed on a rock. She leaned forward. "Terry, this is your skill, your job, your opportunity to make your career and your life more interesting and to do something *good*. This will set a standard for everyone who is in the trade. Some prices must go up, but we need to stop the *instant* response of price rises all the way."

"Okay. I'll have a go."

"Good. But remember the starting point, your position of power: you have the contract which they signed. Then, let's work together. If necessary, call in all the sub-contractors, and really work together, all pulling in one direction."

He blinked, shocked. Charity smiled. Terry walked out with a slightly detectable unsteadiness. Charity sat back and exhaled. She was feeling unsteady, too. From where exactly had all that come? Apart from her memory of the grizzled old clerk, she had made it all up as she went along. Every bit. Every word. But all of it was what she knew to be true. After all, wasn't it just common sense? Wasn't it reducing a complicated problem to its simplest form?

Was that what she needed to do with her investigation?

CHAPTER EIGHTEEN

"I thought you'd forgotten about me," grumbled Eric when she looked into the store-room,

"Forget about *you*?" she said lightly. "That's not likely."

"Find anything?"

"No. Difficult with interruptions every few minutes. I suspect that the original intention was to expose me, but now I'm earning my money as an office manager." She wrinkled her brow. "That's a thought. I've arranged *your* payment terms, but nothing has been said about *mine*."

Eric laughed. "Great businesswoman you are."

"Well, I was thinking about the investigation, and about helping Bernie ..."

"And forgot about yourself. What a dope. Hey! You'll still be paying me?"

"For what? Sitting here, reading and playing games?" But as he wrinkled his nose, she added, "Relax, avaricious nephew. I'll give you something. And we'll have whatever you want for tea tonight."

"Takeaway?"

"The great culinary aspiration for every adolescent. The takeaway. The great treat, the great reward, the great celebration."

"Well, what do you suggest?"

"Whatever will make you happy. I just wanted to say my piece. Don't let me put you off."

"I won't."

"Good."

"And afterwards, instead of crouching over the computer, you could watch a vampire film with me."

"You make it sound like the healthy option. Don't just crouch over your computer: spread yourself out on the settee and watch a vampire film."

"It probably *is* better for you."

"I'm investigating a murder."

"A vampire film might give you an idea."

She let out a sigh which contained a vague 'yeah-hmm'. "It's middayish, Do you want to go somewhere for lunch?"

With a superior air, he said, "I'm having something delivered. A young lady called Linda is treating me to a chicken baguette."

"Oh, very nice. You didn't think of sending her my way, then."

"I assumed that as the office manager, you'd have all that organised. Anyway, I think it was just a favour for me because I'm a cute little guy. She's brought me drinks twice, too."

"O-kay. Well, so long as you're happy, I'll see what the vending machine has to offer, and crack on with the case."

She was standing in front of the vending machine,

staring pensively at it, when Marie passed. "Not much there, I'm afraid, unless you're into toffee-filled milk chocolate. Your best bet is The Sandwich Place, in the next unit. But don't even think about it at this time. They'll be queueing out the door. We order in the morning and pop out well before lunchtime to collect it."

Charity said, "Do you remember all that information you gave me this morning? Well, you missed item number one: where and how to obtain lunch."

"There are other places, but you need to drive to them."

"It's all right. My son has requested a takeaway meal for tonight, so I'll let my body have a rest."

Back at her desk, Charity pondered. She, Charity, seemed to have disappeared and been replaced by Caroline Holt. Was her personality so weak that she had become absorbed into this character who didn't exist? All morning, she had been dispensing advice on matters about which she knew almost nothing. Always, instinctively, she reduced every problem to the simplest form that she could see, and then offered sensible advice or gave a sensible instruction.

Every time that anyone spoke to her in this firm, she immediately became Caroline Holt.

But was Caroline Holt a part of *her*, or was *she* a part of Caroline Holt?

Another question: would it be beneficial to conduct the investigation as Caroline Holt? Rather as Dr Watson used to be guided by asking what Holmes would do, should she ask what Caroline would do?

She put it to the test. She became Caroline Holt. The first thing, Caroline thought, is that she kept looking for specific names and wanting clues to appear, clearly identifiable. Instead, she should be learning about the business, learning about the company. The big background. Somewhere in there would be the first small steps to murder, and the motive.

She remembered a training film in her early office days, a very impressive one about a fire in a busy and crowded research centre. The film started with the aftermath of the fire, the wrecked building, the disfigured members of staff and so on; and then it went back through all the seemingly trivial events which had led to the devastating fire. Someone put something down for a moment, someone didn't do something that he or she was supposed to do, someone thought that something could be done in a few moments; on and on, a trail of seemingly insignificant decisions, leading to the fire.

She opened the folder which contained the contracts. The paper versions, if there were any, would have been better. You can insert fingers and strips of paper into pages, there are scribbled notes, and it's easier to dart forwards and backwards. However, she didn't want to draw attention to her curiosity by going down asking for files. Her role was temporary office manager, not auditor.

Refusing to sigh, she selected the first contract and began to read.

Three hours later, she needed coffee reinforcements. So much repetition of the old routine. The subcontractors submitted optimistic dates and prices, then blamed *their* subcontractors; PH in turn did exactly the same. Everyone lied to win contracts, then blamed their suppliers, the government, the war in the east, an epidemic somewhere affecting animals or people, the weather, the price of fuel. No-one ever admitted a mistake, apologised, and accepted that it was covered by the contingency payments. Everyone lied, everyone cheated, and everyone passed the cost up to the next level in the supply chain, all the way to the buyer.

There were many complex financial reasons for inflation. Here was a simple one.

She told herself that, okay, she understood the system, there were surely too many people at it for it to justify a murder, and one more contract would be a reasonable point at which to stop this bit of background research.

Just one more.

PH Developments and Luckham Council. Hmm. That had potential. Commercial corruption and council corruption often combined to make the sort of big thing that thousands of people would complain about if they had someone to take any notice.

Even before the terms and conditions, the contract was obscure, even mysterious. The schedule of work stated that the work would be in accordance with various annexes, which weren't with the contract documents. And no price was shown. So, a schedule of work with no work and no prices. Good start. Then, PH and the council settled into a joint exercise in obfuscation, in which the council were thoroughly adept. They were all from The Department of Environmental Development. It was like reading a succession of those planning applications that are tied to lampposts, which state that in accordance with ... pursuant to ... clause 9(iii), sub-clause 43(v), in variance of paragraph 19(vi) sub-section 43(ii). All you have to do is spend seventeen hours in the council offices, requesting clarification of the appropriate regulations, to find that someone wants to demolish an eighteenth century cottage and replace it with a cube of concrete and steel.

However, she reminded herself, reading a dull contract and having grumbly thoughts weren't going to help the investigation. A quick look through the correspondence, then something else.

The emails were short and almost all were merely referring to an attachment, which was no longer attached. Missing annexes, missing attachments, a missing dead body. Was there a connection?

Well, she certainly wasn't going to find it by looking at electronic copies of contracts and their correspondence. And this was not doing her brain any good. It was all so dull. All to Mr Henry from various people working in the council's environmental development plan for a sustainable future. Oh. Really? What did that even mean?

Well, let Charity be baffled; that wasn't Caroline's way.

The information which you want is what is missing. Not just the information itself: its absence is vital information.

One more email before trying something else.

Dear Tom

Very informal. It shows what you can do when you're hand in glove.

With reference to our discussion, I agree that a meeting would be very beneficial.

Yawn.

Regards,
  Susan Frankland.

Environmental Development Plan Manager.

But above the official name and title, the informal name of the person who was writing to Tom.

Suzy.

Bingo.

CHAPTER NINETEEN

"No, sorry, she's on leave," said the anonymous voice.
"Oh. When will she back?"

"That's confidential."

"And her being on leave isn't?"

"May I ask who's calling?"

"Yes, you may. And have. And I'll answer. My name is Caroline Holt, temporary office manager at PH Developments. I'm ringing about contract number PH/TH/422. The person who was dealing with this here is on leave, and his partner is in hospital. I have been called in to keep things moving, and I'm working my way through the current contracts, which makes me rather busy, and very keen not to have unnecessary delays. Now, Ms Frankland was dealing with this case. Therefore, I need to know when she will be back, and unless that is very soon, I shall need to speak to someone else about the contract."

Don't mess with Caroline.

"I'll see if I can find who's dealing with her cases."

"Thank you."

Suzy had added her extension to the main number, so the long delay was odd. After several minutes, a new voice said, "May I help you?"

"That depends. In her absence on leave, are you dealing with Ms Frankland's contracts?"

"Er, not as such. We are waiting to assess the situation before making any decisions."

"Which situation?"

"Well, Ms Frankland's absence. On leave."

"Mr ...?"

"Tony Creddington."

Such selective informality. "Well, Tony, I know enough about large organisations to know that each person is expected to record everything that is done on a case, in such a way that any colleague can pick up the case and know exactly what is happening. Presumably that is the case with this contract. I want you to tell me what the current position is, and then answer some questions that I have."

"Right. Yes. Could I just confirm that contract number?"

"PH/TH/422."

"Right. Give me a moment."

Charity wondered whether she had stepped in another bit of the mystery or was merely encountering the familiar administrative incompetence and reluctance to accept any responsibility.

Another wait. Another voice. This one belonging to an older man, an old administration warrior.

"May I ask who you are?"

She couldn't be bothered with doing the grammar lesson again. Instead, she said, "I'm still Caroline Holt, still calling on behalf of PH Developments about contract

PH/TH/422. So far, I've spoken to two people and had two long delays. Now, being very busy, I want to make some progress on this."

"Well, what do you want to know?"

Charity was very surprised that this gruff growler, no doubt the sort to make underlings doubt their own worth, had not been a victim of one of the council culls. Even she could discern a chronological misfit. On the other hand, perhaps he was useful for repelling people who might disturb his underlings from outside. Well, it wasn't going to work with her. She certainly wasn't an underling. She was an outerling, and entitled to respect.

"First, I want to know to whom I am speaking. You didn't introduce yourself."

"Orris."

"Horace what?"

"No. My surname is Orris."

"Ah. Right, Mr Orris. Well, as I have already explained to two of your colleagues, I want to know what is the current position of this contract."

"It's current position is on my desk, in front of me."

Hilarious. A little joke to tease the grandchildren. Definitely not a suitable response for Caroline Holt. Or for Charity Shields.

"Then, please open it and tell me what the latest file note states."

"No. That's confidential."

"No, it isn't. My company needs to know. My company is entitled to know."

"Your company is entitled to know the current state of the case. It isn't entitled to know the content of our internal messages."

"Yes, it is. Freedom of Information."

"Yes, but I'm sure you're much too busy to go down that route."

"I'm beginning to think that might be necessary. Now, Mr Orris, please tell me what the current situation is."

"Gladly. The case is under review."

"Mr Orris. This is a commercial business. We have sub-contractors, suppliers, customers, all depending on us to be efficient. Do you wish me to terminate this contract?"

"That wouldn't be a decision for me to make on my own, but I suspect that it is highly unlikely."

"Presumably, you will want to discuss it with Ms Frankland when she returns."

There was a long pause. "I might."

"So what date shall I put on the file for review?"

"That is entirely up to you."

"But obviously, you'll discuss it with her when she returns from leave."

"At some point, no doubt. But as I can't say when that would be, I can't give you a date."

"But we have sub-contractors, waiting for ..."

"No, you don't. Goodbye, Miss Shields."

Horrible man, she thought. So unnecessarily nasty. She was now going to consider him one of the suspects. Of what she didn't know, but she was sure that there was something bad going on with ....

Just a moment. What did he say?

Goodbye, Miss Shields.

CHAPTER TWENTY

It was clear that Marie wanted to be the last to leave the office. Even in her Caroline role, Charity didn't want to antagonise her. It wasn't going to be for long, and she had more important things to think about. Such as how the stranger at the council knew her real name, especially after she had told him her other name.

"That's fine," she said. "Let me know when you're nearly ready to go, and I'll leave, too."

"I'm nearly ready to go now."

"In that case, I'll pack up, collect my son, and go."

"I don't want you to think I'm rushing you."

"Not at all. I don't want you to think I want to stay longer than I need to."

She smiled with an excess of sweetness. But she did want to go home now. She needed to relax, and she needed to think.

Eric had been rehearsing his role of Bored Boy. He looked up at her wearily and said, "I am bored ... out of my mind."

"Thank you for giving me the lean version. Come on. Gather your things, and let's hightail it out of here."

Eric stood and looked at her. "She said, "It's an expression from old cowboy films. Perhaps when horses are doing a fast gallop, they raise their tails."

He shook his head and said, "Let's just go."

As they went down the first steps, she said, "Strange, isn't it, that you can *feel* emptiness."

"I can *hear* it, because no-one's making noise."

"So, you're hearing silence?"

"Sort of."

"And I'm feeling emptiness."

Eric grunted.

Marie was waiting in Reception, ready to leave. Charity smiled at her and said, "I'll see you tomorrow, Marie."

"Goodnight, Caroline."

Was that a slight pause between the two words? She was in that sort of mood when you just want to leave the shop. Yes, it's lovely; let's go.

"What's the plan for tonight?" Eric asked.

"You will have a shower, then I shall have a shower. I'll eat what you eat, unless it's something unbearable. Then, I shall give my brain a little while in which to prove its worth. If it fails that test, I shall join you and watch a film which doesn't require any brain function. So, any one of yours."

"Mine are high quality. You should read the reviews sometime."

"Hmm. Well, I need to concentrate on the traffic now, which means not even thinking about the investigation."

"If you need help, just ask."

"I need help. And I need to talk. And listen. Before tea,

when we're tired because we need food, or after tea, when we're tired because we've had food?"

"Before everything. Shower, food, film."

"Right. My choice, too."

By the time she'd darted, braked and wriggled through the rush hour traffic, she wasn't exactly fresh and alert, but she was fuelled by need. She put down her briefcase and directed Eric to a seat. Standing, pacing, like a lecturer, she went through the main points.

"I'm not going to link them all yet," she began. "That will be the second step. First, I want to set them out.

"One, a dead body, possibly Tom Henry of PH Developments.

"Two, no dead body, still possibly as stated.

"Three, a dead sheep.

"Four, a local farmer who impresses with his apparent interest in preservation, but who wants to sell his land and his sheep for the building of houses.

"Now, some new stuff. Five, a contract between PH and the local council with virtually no information in the documents.

"Six, evasion and offensiveness from the local council.

"Seven, the nasty and evasive council official knew who I was. Knows who I am.

"Have I missed anything?"

"Mr Pocket's accident, after the farmer put something in his drink."

Charity spread her arms. "Of all the idiots. A very important thing. Well done, Eric."

She clapped her hands. "Right. Now, tell me, as an eleven year old schoolboy, not as a top detective, do you see more than coincidences in that list?

"Yes. Especially when you put them all together."

"Yes. And, *and*, the man who chased us, after we found the body. Another one for the list. So, that's a 1a and a 3a. And of course, there is all the Bernie background. His wife and Tom, and the note from Suzy, who might be a woman at the council who …"

Charity!" Eric said with eleven year old sternness. "You need to stop babbling, create a document, and write a proper list, linking the different parts."

"You're right. But I suspect there will be so much linking that I'll end up with a list which is barely visible behind linking loops."

"Isn't there an app, or something that can do it for you?"

"A detection linking tool? If there were, do you think I'd be able to use it?"

"Well, if you're not up to it, call in a real detective. A man."

Charity gave him a look cold enough to shrivel mustard. "You go and have your shower, and I'll do my list, with all its links."

"You'd better show me how to operate the shower."

"I'm sure there's irony in there somewhere, but I'm too tired to work it out. Come along."

After she explained the shower's idiosyncracies, Eric said, "So, really, you don't know how to make it work."

"I know how to make it work. I don't know how to make it work satisfactorily."

"Which means that in the middle of my shower, the water might suddenly turn cold."

"Yes. I recommend having the dial on medium. Less of a shock. And better for your skin."

"It doesn't matter. If that water turns cold, I'll run a mile."

"That's fine. Just don't do it near me."

Eric continued to look as though he was afraid the shower was going to attack him. Charity said, "You go and prepare. Off with the dirty clothes, take your clean clothes to the shower. I'll set it running, then depart. Keep the shower door shut while you're washing. I don't want the floor to be under one big puddle."

After that had been sorted, she set to work on her document, adding the previously missed items. Then she made another list under the heading 'Links and Inferences'.

Dead body linked to dead sheep.

Dead sheep linked to farmer.

Farmer linked to Bernie's accident.

Farmer linked to the building of houses on his land.

Dead body (when alive) linked to the council.

Dead body (when alive) linked to Suzy.

Suzy linked to the council.

There was also the dead body (when alive) link to Bernie's wife

"Finished!" called Eric.

"That was quick."

"I'm a quick washer."

"I don't doubt that. The speed of drying implies the speed of washing. However, I'll have to take your word for it. You select a film while I have mine."

"What about tea?"

She groaned. "I forgot about that."

"Like Sherlock Holmes. Absorbed in the case."

"Very good, Eric. Another speck of light in the gloom."

"Is it?"

"Yes. And as a treat, we'll have takeaway."

"Great choice. I'll order. Same as last time?"

"You remember what I had last time?"

"Oh, yes."

"Right, then. Order away. I'll go and have a shower."

Unlike Eric, she took her time over showers, beginning with the selection of clothes. It wasn't a case of style or fashion: she almost had personal relationships with her clothes, even the shabbiest items. Sometimes, she wore something simply because she hadn't worn it for a while, and she thought it might feel rejected.

For a change, the water wasn't in its frivolously fluctuating mood, and she was soon in that relaxed state in which having lathered herself once, she went round again, just for the pleasure, eyes closed, warm and soapy water pouring down her.

"Charity."

She squealed and leapt back, hitting her head on the shower hook, and aimed a jet of water at the shower screen, trying to blur the transparency.

"What?" she yelled.

"The food's arrived, and he needs to be paid."

"I'll be out in a moment. Go away."

She let out a combined sigh and groan. Of course she couldn't just have a peaceful shower without having to wrap a towel round and go and pay for food, *after* being stared at by that opportunist little oik.

She didn't need a murder case to shred her nerves.

CHAPTER TWENTY-ONE

Charity wasn't in the best of moods when she arrived at her little desk. The previous evening had left her sluggish in body and mind. A pizza which kept resisting her attempts to swallow, to the accompaniment of a film which consisted of cops, certainly not policemen, wearing tee shirts and jeans, shooting other people in tee shirts and jeans, and constantly arguing with one another and scoffing noodles and burgers from friendly street traders.

The journey to PH Developments had been horrible, one long jerky traffic jam.

And when you arrive, late and in a foul mood, you really don't want to see that you're the last one in and when you sit down hear someone say, "Oh, you're here. We were about to ring."

"Yes," Charity replied with savage pleasantness. "I was stuck in a traffic jam. Clearly, like Truman's rain, it was a traffic jam just for me and none of the other staff here. While you're here, Marie, what do you know about contract number PH/TH/422?"

"I don't know if off the top of my head."

"It's making me curious because there is a schedule of work which refers to annexes which aren't there and…."

"Probably a template," Marie said abruptly. "We have a lot of those. Basically, you fill in the gaps. It saves a lot of time writing out repetitious parts."

Charity sat nodding as though taking this in. Then she said, "As I was about to say, and the council people were extremely evasive and uncooperative, to the point of offensiveness."

"Oh? I *am* surprised. I've always found them extremely cooperative."

"With whom do you usually deal at the council?"

"Oh, different people for different contracts."

"Susan Frankland?"

"Possibly. The name doesn't ring a bell."

"Mr Orris?"

"Again. I might have dealt with him at some point. The name doesn't stand out."

"So, cooperation all the way, names not sticking because no-one caused any trouble."

"Yes, I suppose."

"Well, I must have been unlucky. One after another, two evasive, and the third evasive and abusive. It makes me wonder why. Doesn't it make you wonder why?"

"Well, we all have bad days."

Charity looked at her for several seconds. "Yes, we do, Marie. And I'm no exception. I'm having one now." She exhaled it away and asked, "How are things going in the rest of the office? Any problems?"

"Nothing we can't deal with."

"Hmm. Well, an office manager needs to know how the

members of the department are dealing with problems. When Mr Henry and Mr Pocket are here, do you provide reports for them?"

"As you know, Mr Pocket was concerned with marketing, so was rarely involved in the administration side of things. Mr Henry and I used to work closely on matters of importance."

"Well, now you're going to work closely with me. Keep me informed of progress and problems. You may do this with written reports, or you may book some time with me for discussions. Or both. I'll leave it to you."

She looked at her computer screen, even though she hadn't switched on yet, as a way of dismissing Marie. Firm, decisive action, until she had a sudden, late, thought.

"Used to?" she called after Marie.

"I'm sorry?" Marie said, turning back.

"You said that you and Mr Henry *used to* work closely."

Marie shrugged and smirked casually. "I suppose because we've been given no idea of when he'll return, and you're here and firmly in charge."

"Of course. It just confused me for a moment. I thought perhaps I'd missed something."

"No, nothing like that." This was followed by a polite laugh.

Charity stared at the empty doorway. Another one for the list, in the links and inferences. She wasn't going to allow any coincidences. Everything meant something.

But one troubling thing was this: would all the linked parts combine into one enemy? Say, a trio of Roger McCarthy, Orris, and Marie. A corrupt landowner, a corrupt council official, and a corrupt employee of PH Developments.

And how about this for a trio of victims: Tom Henry, murdered, Bernie Pocket, almost murdered, and a meddling young lady called Charity?

With spectacularly bad timing, someone suddenly appeared in the doorway.

"Hello," said the sudden appearer. "Sorry to bother you. If it's convenient, I've brought the stats."

"Statistics? Just tell me where to sign. But first, who are you?"

"Sorry. Linda Coles. I work in the main office."

"Have a seat."

"Thank you."

Charity did a quick assessment. Linda was still young... ish, but had apologised herself into early middle age. She seemed to have a permanent stoop of subservience. She even seemed reluctant to look at Charity.

"How are the statistics?"

Linda looked at Charity's chin. "Everyone seems to be happy with them, but they still need to be checked for any errors."

"Do *you* check them, or are you just the messenger?"

"I do the final check before they are passed to Mr Henry or Mr Pocket."

"Do they find many errors?"

"Er, no. Not many."

"Any?"

"Er, not that I recall."

"Do they check for errors?"

"I don't know."

"Do *you* find errors?"

"Some. Occasionally."

"And what do you do?"

"I put them right."

Charity was in full Caroline mode, but with a dash of Charity emotion.

"That's a big responsibility, isn't it?"

"Er …"

"And what is your position in the firm?"

"General Administration."

"That's not a position; that's an area. What is your position in General Administration?"

"I don't know."

"Then what are your duties?"

"Well, bits of everything. Anything that needs doing, I suppose."

Without missing the irony, Charity saw the potential usefulness of Linda. Trying not to sound devious, she said, "Presumably, you would know where to find a contract file if I wanted it."

"Oh, yes. They're all in the file room."

"Oh. That wasn't on my induction tour. Where is it?"

"Top floor, next to the store room."

"So, if I asked you to fetch a contract file, you'd have no trouble finding it."

"No. I'm very careful about numbering and filing. And I keep a list of every file and what it's about."

Charity felt like a cobra, pulling back to strike. "And what is PH/TH/422 about?"

"I can't tell you about that one. It's one of the confidential contracts. Ms Ridings keeps those in a special cabinet."

"Are the confidential contracts included in the statistics?"

"No."

"Then the statistics are always wrong, and of little, or no, value."

"Er ..."

Charity could see danger signs on both sides of the road as she said, "Do you have access to those files?"

"Oh, no. Only Ms Ridings has that."

"And, I presume, Mr Henry and Mr Pocket."

"Oh. Yes, I suppose so."

Charity spoke slowly, her words slightly ahead of her thoughts. "Linda, let's assume that for whatever reason, Ms Ridings isn't here today. I, office manager, have an urgent need to see that contract. How can I do it?"

"There's a spare copy of every key. They're all in a tin in my drawer, which I keep locked."

"And what do you do with the key to the tin?"

"It's kept in a secret place."

"WHICH SECRET PLACE?"

"It wouldn't be secret if I told you." Linda was close to tears. Charity knew that she must control her frustration, or she wouldn't make progress. And it wasn't Linda's fault. She was sticking to the simple policy of keeping a secret secret.

"Linda, what would happen if you were unexpectedly absent?"

"Ms Ridings knows where the key is kept."

"Yes. And if Ms Ridings were also unexpectedly absent? You see, this is the problem with security. Complete security means that no-one has access to anything. Burglars, staff, management, all locked out of the system."

"And Mr Henry has a full set."

Trying to stay calm and detached, Charity said, "Ah. That's more like it. Okay, Linda. Interrogation over. I like to be sure that I understand systems. And usually at my level, there aren't files which are too confidential to be seen. I'm representing the top two people in this company. So, being told there are passwords which I'm not to know, files which I'm not to see, and a security system which has had to be painstakingly explained to me, are combining to irritate me a little. But I think I'm satisfied now. You've been very help-ful. Thank you.

"As for the statistics, I'm going to do as Mr Pocket does. I'll sign for them and take full responsibility. Thank you again."

Linda emanated relief when she received the papers. She looked alarmed again when Charity said, "When you're downstairs again, please ask Ms Ridings to pop up."

"Er ..."

"Yes?"

"Er ... I think it would be better if you asked her."

Charity understood. "All right."

"And she might not like my talking about ..."

"The office security system? How strange. There seems to be a distinct lack of teamwork in this place. But I'm a team player and shall do my best to keep you out of any conversations on that topic. Obviously, you'll avoid the subject, too."

"Thank you."

When Linda had gone, Charity rang Marie's extension and asked her to pop up. She stared at her computer, not really seeing anything. She didn't want to have this talk with Marie, but she needed to, and not just for the investigation. A business shouldn't be run on secrecy and fear.

But how to explain that and insist on it, with firmness and tact? This wasn't her company, and she wasn't a real office manager.

Charity stepped aside. This was definitely a task for Caroline Holt.

When she saw Marie in her doorway, she continued to look at her computer screen and said, "Hi, Marie. Have a seat."

She sat back and looked at her adversary. Now, that she knew about the other set of keys, this was now almost a matter of principle. But Marie was looming over everything as a sort of office manager by default. This could be a test case.

She said, "I'm a bit confused, Marie. I'm here to represent Mr Henry and Mr Pocket. In doing that, I intend to try very hard to keep the business going as it would if they were here. To a large extent, that means letting those with the necessary experience and skills carry on working as usual. However, that does not mean sitting back and ignoring everything so long as it all seems to be running smoothly. Even when I don't intend to interfere, it is important that I know what is going on."

"I understand that Linda brought the stats up a little while ago."

"Yes, she did. Sheets of numbers. That is not what I mean. Let me give you an example of what I mean. A hypothetical case. I have stayed late one night. I am the only person in the place. An irate managing director rings me to ask what the hell is going on with a certain contract. I tell him that I don't know. Well, he asks, is there anyone there who *does* know? No. I'm the only one here. Well, who are you? The office manager. At this point, he moves on from being irate to being furious and contemptuous."

"I'm sure none of our contractors would behave in that manner."

Charity leaned forward and spoke slowly. "It was an example, Marie, of my needing to know about a contract and my not knowing about a contract."

"Well, in normal circumstances, you wouldn't be here on your own, and there would be a member of your staff to …"

"NO!" It was almost a shout. "I refuse to be in the position of having to say to a contractor or government official that one of my staff will brief me on the case and I'll ring him or her back. I need to know."

"Well, the files are all on the computer system."

"But they aren't, are they? On the computer, contract number PH/TH/422 looks like a template, with no task, no prices, no dates. But the paper file is in a special cabinet of confidential contracts."

"Miss Holt. Do you have security clearance for your work here?"

"I have Bernie clearance."

"There are proper ways of doing things."

"Take that up with Bernie."

"Why are you so keen to see that contract?"

"Because people are so keen for me not to see it. I want access to that cabinet. Of all the files that I need to know about, those are obviously the most important."

"They are confidential for a reason."

"Just one reason? The same one for every contract?"

There was a brief pause for thought. Then, "I can pull out that particular contract for you, but I'll need a little time."

"Why?"

"To ensure that nothing that shouldn't be seen isn't left in the papers."

"Office manager."

"Head of admin. Responsible for office security."

"I want to see that contract file."

"You will. After I have carried out my security check."

Charity sat back, feigning resignation. She had taken it as far as she wanted. She had measured Marie's determination to protect the contents of the file. What would she gain by seeing a file which had been stripped of the important information? What she needed was to find the other set of keys.

She shook her head in resignation. "Never mind for now. I'm sure it can wait until Mr Henry and Mr Pocket return. After all, I'm here for only a few days."

"Yes," Marie agreed, letting her pleasure shine out of her eyes.

CHAPTER TWENTY-TWO

"I've been a fool," Bernie said. "The age-old defence, I suppose. I did my job and left other people to do theirs. I was the one who did the patter, the persuading, drew them in, then, in effect, handed them over to Tom and his team back at base. I wasn't interested in the technical stuff, negotiations over prices, dates, risk management, any of that. While they were all bogged down in that, I was off to the next one."

Charity said, "Now that I've told you things, can you look back and see things that you missed at the time?"

"Such as Tom and my wife?"

"That, for one. But most people miss those things until afterwards and the penny drops, But how about Tom and your wife connecting to whatever is going on at PH?"

He frowned in ponderment, sighed a few times, deep-ended and darkened the frown, did one big sigh, and said, "Right. I've gone back, like the traditional drowning man, seeing the last few months passing before me. Yes, I think there have been a lot of clues, which this thick and always rushing marketing manager kept missing. Well, not so much missing, as not taking in and considering. Little things, superficially, individually, perhaps big in the new context. I often thought that Marie seemed to be in charge, and Tom was taking orders from her. It's a difficult one. I've seen this sort of thing before. Some men need to be organised, even bullied. Often it brings efficiency, and often I think it fulfils a sort of need in men to be controlled, and in women to do the controlling."

"Did she organise you?"

"She tried to, but not very hard. Bear in mind that you are seeing me after my wife's infidelity, my partner's murder, a mystery woman, and a very bad car accident. A lot of salesman's bounce has been knocked out of me in different ways. I wasn't in the office much, and when I was, I was always on the move, talking to several people at once, doing the patter, gulping coffee, having a session with Tom when he was in. If Tom had been sitting at his desk with a knife in his chest, it would have taken me ten minutes to notice it."

Charity smiled. This was one salesman who could assess himself and honestly acknowledge his defects. Or skills, depending on how you looked at it.

But Bernie was warming up now. "I think Marie is an important figure in all this. You must find a way of looking at that contract, and probably others. First, throw her right off the scent. Find a way of telling her that you've lost interest in it. Tell her that I've told you not to interfere in that side of things. That'll please her. No, I'll do it. I'll call her, perhaps be slightly disparaging about you, tell her that

I'll be back in a few days, which I hope is true, and that I'll be relying on her to keep everything running smoothly. You settle into a vague consultancy role, detached, aloof, as though you really don't care anymore."

Charity nodded. "Yes. It won't be pleasant, but I think you're right."

Bernie was still thinking, his brain trying to atone for the wasted years. He said, "On the other hand, there's a small back door, not included in the security system. Tom and I wanted to have our own little access. I have the key."

Charity tilted her head. "Ye—s?"

"It might already be too late , of course, but we must try."

"We?"

"Well, yes. You and I, in our different roles. I'm doing the planning, and you'll be doing the, er...."

"Difficult and dangerous bit."

"Well, yes, I suppose you could call it that."

"I do call it that. I'm to go in through the back door, grope my way through all the corridors to Tom's office, find the keys, grope my way to the confidential files office ..."

"Yes, all of that, "Bernie said impatiently. "But let's drop the verb 'grope'."

"It's going to be pitch black, Bernie. Suggest some suitable verbs."

"Don't you have a torch?"

"Yes."

"How powerful?"

"About three glowworms power."

"Well, the darker it is, the brighter it'll seem."

"Salesmen are born, not made. We're discussing my

difficult and dangerous task, and you're giving me the old patter."

"Only because I think it's the best way. If you go in worrying and nervous, you'll make mistakes. Go in, up the stairs to Tom's office, find the keys, go to the cabinet, open it, remove that contract, lock the cabinet and leave."

"Yes, that sounds good. And I like to be positive. But may we settle for a few moments on 'find the keys'?"

"Tom wasn't the imaginative, creative sort, so the keys should be easy to find. They're probably in one of his desk drawers."

"Was Tom the first manager in the history of office administration to leave his office door *and* his desk drawers unlocked?"

"I do have a key to his office. In my jacket pocket, in the cupboard there."

"And the drawers?"

"They'll either be unlocked or … you'll need to open them."

"You mean prise them open with my jemmy?"

"Do you have one?"

"No. Will a chisel do?"

"Probably. Modern office furniture isn't built to last. It shouldn't be a problem, provided that you do it the right way."

"You remind me of my Uncle Ken."

"Let's go through it again," Charity said, trying to talk up some courage in the lay-by opposite PH Developments.

Somehow, the vivid light from the streetlamps seemed to emphasise the darkness in which they were sitting.

Eric said, "I know what to do. I watch the building and everything around it. If I hear or see anything that might be someone going into the building, I give you three rings."

"That's it. Last check: powered-up and a signal?"

"Yes. You?"

"Good point. Yes, to both."

"Right." She took a deep breath. "Here I go. Keep your doors locked. I'll be as quick as I can."

She opened the door and slid out. A last look round, then she scurried across the road, over the little car park, and round the back. She inserted the key, pushed the door open and, recognising the point of no return, stepped inside and closed the door.

The darkness was intense, feeling thickly oppressive, menacing. She switched on the torch. One of the glow-worms had left. The beam, more a whisper of pale light, improved her view of the darkness for a few inches in front of her. She would have to grope, after all.

Bernie had given her instructions and drawn a simple diagram, which lacked both artistic and draughtsmanship merit. She already had a very rough idea of rooms and passages from the front part, but she hadn't even known about this route from the back. There was nothing for it but to keep feeling her way while remembering what she could of Bernie's drawing.

She pushed open a door. Two doors so far, and so far, so good. The thought was just a nervous twitter, and she knew it. Another door, then a left turn and the stairs. Right. This was now familiar. Up two flights, then turn right, another door, and Tom's office should be the second on the left.She tried the handle and was pleased to find that the door was locked; perhaps that meant no-one had been in there looking for keys. She used Bernie's other key to open it. A moment later, she was in the office of the dead man who had set all this mystery going.

Was this going to be the big, breakthrough event? The thought encouraged her. She felt her way round the desk, and took out her chisel. This was it: the moment when she became a criminal.

"Oh, just do it!" she muttered, and shoved the chisel blade into a thin gap.

The drawer opened. For the simple reason that it wasn't locked. She didn't even pause to slap her forehead. This was a time to focus on the task. She pushed the chisel down into the deep front pocket of her trousers and began the search.

The first drawer was mostly stationery items, but in the second drawer was a bunch of keys. Which was good, but this was unsettlingly easy. The keys that she wanted in an unlocked drawer? After all that secrecy and intransigence about access?

Focus! She had a quick look through all the drawers, hoping to see some important correspondence, but doing this by the light of her dim, and dimming, torch, wasn't a suitable time.

She closed the drawers, locked the door and went back to the stairs. On the third floor, she walked as quickly as she could in the darkness, noticing that the little torch was now providing nothing more than a pale yellow glow. She turned it off. She might need that weak glow later. But she doubted it.

Slightly familiar territory, past the store room, then the file room. It was locked, but the seventh key opened it. She gave the torch one last chance, switching it on and holding it out as though it had magic powers. In front of her, she saw four metal cabinets, looking like dormant robots in an Asimov story. Swinging the torch round, she saw another cabinet to her right, standing at a right angle to the others. Above was a small skylight, matching the one in the store room.

She checked the lock, knowing that only certain keys would fit it. She tried the most likely one. It turned.

Her telephone rang. One, two, three.

Faintly, in the depths of the building, she heard a door open and close.

She hesitated. She was seconds away from having the file, but in seconds her escape might be cut off.

To hide, then escape, was the priority.

But where?

She locked the cabinet and went to the open door. The footsteps were coming up the stairs, already on the floor below. A powerful torch beam shone like a searchlight. The blinding sort that made people stand motionless.

A man's voice called, "We know you're in here. We've been expecting you. It was a trap, and you're trapped."

Charity was almost paralysed by her fear, her dread of this slowly advancing enemy.

Leaving the door open, she went to the end of the passage and crouched. She had one, small plan. She couldn't think of anything else.

The torch beam came up the stairs, the steady footsteps just behind. At the top of the stairs, the light showed the open door. Now, the walk was fast, into the room.

Moving quickly on tip-toe, Charity went almost as far as the open door, then vaulted over the banister.

Her intention was to land lightly, silently, on the stairs. It was a failure. Her body was angled wrongly. The stairs reverberated.

There was a shout above her.

In one movement, she struggled to her feet and ran down the stairs. For a moment, the torch from above shone directly on her, then flickered as the enemy hurtled after her.

"Cut her off!" was called from above.

"I'll stop her," replied a woman's voice from below. That was a mistake. Now, Charity knew roughly where the lower person was. And running downstairs gave her one big advantage. She leapt and kicked, karate style. Both feet connected with a chest. The other person staggered backwards and clattered down the rest of the stairs.

Charity longed to run to the car, but the man was close behind her, and she didn't want to involve Eric.

And in a place in her mind which was beyond terror was the stubborn determination not to leave without the file.

At the bottom of the stairs, she turned left, through a door, along a passage, through another door, and into the main office. She hoped.

Absurdly, it now occurred to her to wonder why the hunters hadn't turned on the lights. Did *they* need darkness, too? Were *they* concealing *their* identities?

Trying to defer the inevitable, she stumbled through desks, into an open channel through the middle. Knowing that in the end, it would make little difference, she felt a desk, went round it, squeezed past the chair and crouched in the leg space.

The door opened.

The searchlight beam from the torch began its inspection. First the broad sweep of the room. Next would be the inspection of each place in which she could hide. Under a desk was on the same quality level as under the bed.

The steps and the beam advanced slowly to the accompaniment of a psychological attack. "Charity. We know who you are and why you're here. It's time to admit defeat and go out of our lives and back to yours. Nothing will happen to you, provided that you mind your own business."

Crouched in the darkness, with the menacing serpent of light wriggling and coiling round the room in search of her, she was the terrified prey, hiding in her small space, knowing that at any moment, she would be dazzled into paralysis. Then, human hands would seize her.

What was there left for her to do but attack?

At exactly the right moment.

The bright light was showing her glimpses of where the desks and spaces were. She remembered that when she squeezed into her hiding place, the chair had moved smoothly on little wheels. If she pushed it into a gap, its sudden appearance could reveal where she was, but it might distract him for vital seconds.

The door opened again, and a harsh voice called, "You vicious bitch! I'm going to kill you!"

The man called, "I've been trying to persuade her."

"Never mind that! She's trapped. I'll wait by the door in case she makes a break for it. You flush her out."

So, that was clear.

She needed a weapon.

She *had* a weapon.

She removed the chisel from her pocket. It wasn't her

weapon of choice. She wasn't sure that she could chisel someone.

With a cold acceptance of reality, she knew what to do.

With no attempt at subtlety, she pushed the chair. It rolled a few feet and stopped.

"Found her," called the man. To Charity, he said, "Come on, girl. No-one's going to harm you."

"No. I don't trust you. You *will* harm me. Just leave me alone."

"I promise you won't be harmed."

"No!"

"Just grab her!" shrieked the voice from the door.

Charity cowered in the small space as the man bent down, put his torch down and reached in.

This was her moment.

Three times, she shoved the chisel into his face. He screeched and retreated. She crawled out, picked up the torch, did one last jab, then headed for the door. Now, the blinding light was hers. "Your turn now," she yelled.

The door opened and closed. When Charity opened it again, she heard the other predator running rapidly away, up the stairs and along the passage. Moments later, a door closed.

From behind, the man called, "The police are on their way. You'd better have a good story for them."

"In that case, I'll stay here," Charity replied. "I do have a good story for them."

"Just clear off. And keep your mouth shut and your nose out. That's a warning."

She thought of going back up for the file, but she couldn't face any more struggles in the dark. On the other hand, she didn't want all the incriminating documents to be removed.

It was time to introduce a little calm.

"Understood," she said.

She was ready to go home.

CHAPTER TWENTY-THREE

E ric was excited about Charity's dramatic account, but a little disappointed that he hadn't been involved.

"But you were," Charity explained, sipping her wine, nibbling her toast. "You had one vital job to do, and you did it. While I had little in the way of a plan, and was improvising wildly, you stuck exactly to the plan. You observed, gave me three rings, and waited. If you'd become bored and stared at your iPad and not seen those people arriving, I'd have been too busy searching through files to notice until it was too late. And if you'd come in, you'd have complicated things, and might have become a hostage."

"And you attacked that guy with a chisel. Wow."

"It's not really a wow, Eric. I'm not proud of it. I'd have preferred to think my way out of the problem."

"You did! You were crouched under a desk and you'd been caught. You thought about ways out of the problem and there was just the one. I mean, did you really believe they were going to let you go? Promise you won't tell. I promise. Okay, off you go. As you said, one murdered, one nearly murdered. And you probably ticked all the boxes in the competition for next murder victim."

"You're very articulate when it suits you. You just need the right motivation. Such as a discussion about murder and stabbing someone with a chisel. Anyway, as I keep saying, I just lashed out in a panic. Just a frightened, girl. Like the ones in the films who grab a pair of scissors and stab the man who's … trying to kill her."

"Have his wicked way, you mean."

"Well, killing someone is wicked, so yes."

"You might have killed *him* with your chisel attack."

"Chisel defence. Frightened girl, Eric."

"No. Tough detective defeating the bad guys."

She smiled at him. He meant well. It was a nice compliment.

He said, "What's the next step?"

"Ah. Now that is a difficult one. I've already been pondering, and every option seems to be the wrong one. However, my current inclination, as an investigator, and as someone who is determined not to do what they expect me to do, is to go to work tomorrow and act as though nothing has happened."

"Ooh, risky."

"Well, two things. One is that they must be protecting an illegal business arrangement which is bringing in, or will bring in, a great profit. The last thing they want is drama, publicity and police officers."

"That might rule out shooting you, but it still leaves lots of other safe possibilities, such as pushing you downstairs, cutting your brake cables, or electrocuting you. There are lots of ways to kill you."

"So, what would you advise?"

"Go there. Take the risk."

"Okay. That's what we'll do."

"We'll?"

"I'm not going to leave you here all day."

"I could manage."

"Besides which, I need you for the full pretence. Everything is going to be normal. I'll take a normal interest in the work, not be contentious or inquisitive. I might even be a little subdued. You know, that look when people ask are you all right. Resigned. Defeated."

"How shall *I* look?"

She looked at him. "I think that your usual appearance will be in keeping with the mood that I'll be trying to project."

"What does that mean?"

"I mean you haven't concealed from anyone the fact that being left in a store room for about eight hours a day has not encouraged light-hearted enthusiasm in you."

"What is there to be enthusiastic about?"

"Nothing. Which is why I shan't need you to do any acting. Just be your usual fed-up self. In the store room, I mean. I'll pack extra food for you. And more books?"

"I'm still reading the other one."

"Tut. More reading and less … whatever you do on that thing."

"I'm enjoying it. I'm just a slow reader. And there's a lot of old stuff that I don't know."

"That's true. Tomorrow, straight after work, we'll catch the train to the big city, and we'll have a look round the few old bits that haven't been demolished and replaced."

"Oh."

"A little bit of history, Eric. To help you to understand and enjoy old books."

"What about tea?"

"Ah, yes. The food. Well, the city has all your favourite junk food places. So, the usual bribe, Eric."

"Okay. Sounds okay."

"Good. And so to bed."

"Can't I have a bit longer?"

"No. It's already late, and I need to be fresh and alert tomorrow."

"I don't. You go on to bed. I'll see to everything when I'm ready."

"Nice try. No chance. For one thing, I wouldn't let *any* eleven year old boy see to everything after I'd gone to bed. Even the thought makes me shudder. For another, while expecting you to be bored and fed-up, with very little to occupy your mental faculties, I'd like you to leave your mental pilot light on and be surreptitiously observant. Remember that you are my assistant, not just my early warning system. I want you to watch and listen, and be prepared."

She watched that sink in, and was pleased with the effect. He looked ready to start work right now. She added, "And, Eric, you know what your bedtime routine is. I'll leave you to do it. Give me a shout when you've finished in the bathroom."

"*May* I read for a little while?"

"For a little while, provided that it's the Sherlock Holmes book."

"D'oh."

"You can do your own bit of detection work. I have a little plan forming, involving you. In the story, you will find a big clue to what I am thinking of doing, and what you would be doing."

She was enjoying her own little read in bed when Eric reached the clue. His protest came clearly through the bedroom wall.

"Charity! I am *not* a pygmy, and you are mad!"

CHAPTER TWENTY-FOUR

Marie did a very bad job of pretending not to be shocked by Charity's attendance. Charity smiled and said, "Morning, Marie. I need the new password."

"Timbuktookgr9," Marie replied.

"Thank you. Everything progressing as it should be?"

"Yes. I think so."

"Excellent. Well, you know what you're doing, so I'll leave you to keep everything running smoothly. But call me if you need me."

"Right."

Charity turned to her computer. Dismissed, Marie turned away and left. Charity looked at a few bland contracts, then decided to check on Eric. And, as he quickly realised, to do a bit of skylight reconnoitering. He remembered not to blurt anything out and settled for scowling at her. The scowl intensified when she nodded in approval. She gave him a thumbs-up. He rolled his eyes.

At lunchtime, they went to a small landscaped area with wooden tables and benches, for the purpose of office lunches, and apparently some relaxed team meetings. Being round the corner from PH Developments, it also provided a view of the back of the building.

"What do you think?" Charity asked.

"What … what do *I* think?" was the mocking reply.

"Oh, come on now, assistant, partner …"

"Accomplice."

"Very good, Eric."

"Right. How would we go up to the roof?"

That was the big obstacle that she had immediately seen. Yes, there was a drainpipe, and a thin industrial estate tree near to the roof, but no safe means of putting a child up there. And then there was all the rest of the undertaking. Oh, well.

She sighed and said, "It was the best of ideas, it was the worst of ideas." She looked at the office building and said, "I wonder whether this place is the source of the information that I need or a big distraction. A red herring. I'm confident that all the evil emanates from here, but I think I'm in danger of bogging down in what's happening here."

"Why not have a break? Forget about it for a few days."

"You mean forget the murder, the attempted murder, the conservationist farmer who wants to sell his land for a housing estate, the secret documents, the evasive council officials, and whatever they were going to do to me last night? Order a pizza, put on a film and relax?"

"Yes."

She shrugged. "Okay. Just the one night. And provided that …hello."

Eric called, "Where are you going?"

"Just over here. Shush and stay there."

She hurried round the side of the building and stood by

one of the trees, staring at the muddy green Discovery which had stopped outside the entrance. Marie hurried out, glanced right and left and climbed in. As the vehicle moved off, she went back to Eric. He looked at her disapprovingly, knowing that she had reverted to impetuous active mode.

"Okay, Charity. What is it?"

"The cat has popped out. Charity Mouse wants to make it a short lunch break, escort you back to your store room, and perhaps just have a glance at the next room."

He sighed, but stood and went back with her without actually complaining. As they approached the door, she said, "Try not to look suspicious."

"How could I look suspicious? I'm just going to go to my store room."

"Yes, but you know how these things escalate."

"I don't want to be part of any escalation. I'll close my door. You be an escalator if you want."

"No, I said things escalate. I don't escalate them."

"Oh, really?"

"Don't sulk. You're making the stairs vibrate. You're walking like a carthorse. These buildings aren't intended to last for a hundred years."

"Horses don't walk."

"What do they do?"

"Canter, trot, gallop."

"You aren't doing any of those things."

"Well, there you are then."

They reached the landing. There was Eric's room. There was the confidential files room. And there was Linda standing guard. She looked as though she had been fastened to the floor. Charity gently steered Eric into the store room, and approached the previously nervous and timid Linda.

"Hello, Linda. What are you doing?"

"Ms Riding put me on guard."

"To guard the confidential files?"

"Yes. Until we have the ..."

"Locks changed. Oh, well. If that's what you've been told to do, and you're happy to do it, and can be spared from your usual work, carry on. Is this your lunch break?"

"No. I'm to have that when Ms Riding returns."

"After her lunch break, I presume."

"When she comes back."

"Hmm. I think I'll have to review the staffing numbers if we can spare someone to stand and do nothing for a significant part of the day."

"I asked about that. I'll have to stay late to finish my usual work."

"I'll leave you to it, Linda."

As she passed the store room, Eric grinned at her. She took a step inside and looked pointedly at the skylight. Eric frowned. He understood.

Back in her office, she decided that she she needed to be out of this. It was too frustrating. This was Bernie's zone. She needed to investigate elsewhere. She sent a message to him, telling him that Marie had gone off with McCarthy and left a guard outside the confidential files office, and was about to have the locks changed, and telling him that there was little she could do, as an investigator, and as a temporary office manager.

Bernie replied seconds later:

> About to ring you. Usual sudden hospital decision. Out today, back in tomorrow.

> Back in where?

> There. You come in, too, please. We can do a quick handover.

> Okay. But only because you said 'please'.

> I remembered that just in time.

> Ha! Are you going to tell Marie, or shall I?

> I'll do it. You just relax and stay out of trouble.

She had several snappy responses to that last bit, but decided not to use any of them. Keep it simple. Tomorrow, Bernie would relieve her. She was already looking forward to having no more involvement with Marie.

But there was something bothering her. She needed clarification. She rang him.

"Bernie, will you demand access to the confidential files?"

"Well, how we do things will be a part of our continuing strategy, which we'll discuss tomorrow."

"Okay, Bernie. I think I understand what that means. My brain automatically translates officespeak. One last question, because the answer will have a big influence on my strategy preparation."

"Go on."

"Are you afraid of Marie?"

"Yes."

"Very afraid?"

"Terrified."

CHAPTER TWENTY-FIVE

"Right," Charity said. "Are you all set and all clear?"

"I don't touch anything electrical in the kitchen, I don't go out, I don't open the door for anyone."

"Good."

"And if anyone breaks in and murders me, I'm to ring 999 immediately."

"Good joke, bad time. But if you need urgent medical, or other, assistance, call 999. And be coherent."

"It's okay. I *know* what to say to them."

"Okay. I'll be as quick as I can. You've had breakfast, so crisps and juice should be enough to keep you from collapsing. I'll lock the door. If you should need to leave quickly, use a window. I don't expect to be long with the cowardly lion. I doubt that we'll do much in the way of planning. And I'd not put it past Marie to be somewhere where she can hear."

"She might have put a bug in his office."

She considered this and said, "It's a possibility. But I'll

have to assume not; it would be too complicated trying to have a secret conversation with Bernie."

She had a last, pointless look round and said, "I should be back in a couple of hours. Stay there, watch a couple of films, read, play your games, I don't care for the next couple of hours, so long as you stay right there."

"Okay. Don't worry."

"I do. Promise you'll stay there."

"I might have to go to the toilet."

"Obviously. But settee, toilet, settee again. That's your limit. Clear?"

"Yes. Perfectly. Now stop fussing and go. The sooner you go, the sooner you'll be back. But don't rush on my account. I'll be fine. I'm good at it."

"I believe you. Okay. Bye."

"Bye."

She locked the door and hurried to the car. But she drove even more carefully than usual. She had a nephew to think about. She didn't want him to be a temporary orphan.

With Bernie back, there was even less parking space, but blocking people didn't matter because she would be gone soon. She almost ran up the stairs, hoping this would be the last time.

She almost collided with Linda, who was coming down.

"Oops," Charity said. "That was close."

After doing her nervous muttering, Linda asked, "No Eric today?"

"No."

"Oh." She was disappointed. "Not ill, is he?"

"No. I'm not staying for long. A quick chat with Bernie, then I'll be off."

"You're finishing here?"

"Yes. It was always temporary. Just holding the fort until Bernie returned."

"Yes. You did say. Well, please give my ... regards to Eric, and tell him I wish him well. And you, of course."

"Thank you. You, too. And I'll pass the message to Eric."

Charity carried on up, and Linda slowly carried on down.

"Hi, Bernie," she said eagerly, pushing aside her reservations.

Bernie was sitting behind his desk, looking very much like someone who had nothing to do and wasn't going to go looking for anything.

"Hi ... Caroline. Glad that I'm back to relieve you?"

"Oh, yes. I need to be quick because I've left Eric on his own. Much to the disappointment of Linda. I'd never have thought I could make her look more glum than usual, but I think I've done it."

"He's a nice boy, and by all accounts, she leads a solitary life since her mother died."

"If he were mine, I'd let her borrow him now and then. Very sad."

"Don't you live a solitary life?"

"Well, yes. But I enjoy it. She looks like the sort of low-esteem person that needs a parent or a spouse. Or a son."

"You're probably right."

"We can discuss things in more depth later, but shall we do a quick summary and preparation?"

"Fine."

"Shall I close the door?"

"Er, no, that's all right," he replied. He lowered his voice. "It might look suspicious."

"That's not a good start, worrying what the staff might think. In the absence of Tom, you're the owner. You shouldn't be worrying about what people might think if you close your door."

"I'm also trying to help you with the investigation. Making people puzzled and suspicious won't help. We don't want people to be on their guard."

"Yes, I suppose that makes sense."

"And you won't have that moment when you think that someone is listening on the other side of the door."

"Okay. I agree. You won that round. Now, strategy. At least one of your contracts, *your* contracts, is being hidden in the double-locked confidential files. Is there any *acceptable* reason for your not having access to it?"

He looked past her and said with a very bad attempt at casual jollity, "Ah, here's Marie? How are you?"

"Good to have you back, Bernie. I'm fine, and everything is running perfectly, working our way round the obstacles."

Charity felt the comment like a spiteful pinch.

"Good, good," said nervous Bernie. "Any updates?"

"I've sent my report to you, and I took the liberty of provisionally arranging some visits for you. I've done my best to keep Tom's side of things moving, and I've put some things in your basket for you to sign."

"Ah. Excellent. Well done, Marie. Well, I'm just going to do a little handover with Ch..aroline..."

"Charoline?"

"He's learning Italian," Charity said.

"Yes. Sometimes forget. Confuse myself. And when

we've done our handover, normal service will be resumed. Apart from my missing partner. Tom."

Marie's quick look at Charity suggested a suppressed smirk. Charity's look suggested that she was too busy thinking to bother with giving or receiving looks. She waited until Marie's footsteps had receded down the stairs, then shook her head at Bernie.

"I know, I know," he said. "That was terrible. No wonder my wife left me."

Charity spread her arms. "But you're the marketing man. The great persuader. The one who moulds people into being willing customers."

"But that only works when people have an innate desire to be persuaded. It's like, pardon the analogy, the girl who keeps saying *No* when she really means *Yes*."

"I don't pardon the analogy, but I understand your point."

"I bet your young assistant has persuaded you into watching films while eating unhealthy food."

"Yes. It's true. He has, I have. But you're wriggling and squirming, as you were when Marie was here. Is this your company?"

"Mine and Tom's."

"And it looks as though Tom is on permanent leave. Which leaves you in charge."

"Right."

"So, be in charge! Manage. Run. Rule. You must ..."

Her telephone played its annoying tune. Seeing the opportunity for temporary relief, Bernie said, "The way things are, you'd better see what the message is."

She raised her eyes and said, "Okay. But this isn't over."

She read the message and said, "Okay. It *is* over. Either

Eric is more stupid than I thought, or something terrible has happened."

She passed the telephone to Bernie. He read it and said, "I'd go for the more stupid one."

"The way things are, Bernie, I think it's the other one."

CHAPTER TWENTY-SIX

Charity began her drive home at a reckless speed before slowing down. Having an accident wasn't going to help anyone or anything. And she couldn't avoid thinking about other things, so going at a steady speed was the sensible thing to do.

She was clear about one thing: although she couldn't rule out stupidity, she did rule out the possibility that Eric had broken his promise. For one thing, Eric wouldn't go for a walk. He might walk *to* somewhere for something which he needed urgently, but he wouldn't walk for the pleasure of walking. And for another, she trusted him. He wouldn't break his promise.

Therefore, he *hadn't* gone for a walk. And, therefore, someone else had sent that message, or Eric had been made to send it.

But how had the kidnapper entered the house? The front and back doors were locked. The windows were closed. She had checked everything before she left. At least three times. She knew that she must go to the police, but first she'd have a look at the house.

She didn't park in the drive. There might be evidence there. She left the car tilted on the pavement, and stood looking. The people in the houses to the right and left were both working couples, off early, back late. Opposite was the break in the houses, occupied by trees. Someone farther away might have seen something, but door-to-door enquiries were for the police.

There were no marks in the drive, but what did she expect? The kidnappers wouldn't have screeched into the drive, spreading instant alarm and causing the scrutiny of neighbours. There was no scratching round the door lock, and the door was still secured. The front windows were still closed. That left the back, which was a much more likely place. It wasn't a pleasant thought.

She went along the side of the house. The back door was still locked, with no sign of damage. She tried the widows. They were all shut. But unless Eric were playing a very bad joke, and was sitting in the house, watching her suffer, then, something must be open. She inserted her fingers into one of the windows.

It opened.

She unlocked the back door and went round to look. The small wooden bowl in which she kept spare screws and pins was upside down on the floor. Looking at an angle, she could see a smeared hand print on the glass. That settled it. Even if Eric *had* broken his promise, even if he *had* decided to sneak out for a walk, there would be no reason to put his hand flat against the window. Someone had expertly opened it.

Competing with her fear for Eric was the now persistent

thought that she was an utter dud of a child-minder. She hadn't been needed at the PH office today. It was a part of her investigation.

Did her little hobby come before the safety of a child?

It was time to go to the police.

She was dreading it.

She was surprised to see three fully-functioning policemen in the small Luckham station. Two of them were rather eagerly on the point of leaving. Charity had the feeling that she'd spoiled their fun. Then, one recognised her.

"Another dead body?"

"No. A live boy. He's been kidnapped."

"Ah," he said with great condescension. "You do have an exciting time. Well, we're just off out. Lots to do. Police work. But I'll leave you with our desk officer, who will be delighted to help you."

"Thanks a lot," muttered the desk officer. When the other two had left, he looked at Charity with barely suppressed irritation and said, "Right. I'll take your details first."

"No, I'll take yours. Name and number, please."

"Police Officer Quigley. 7982.

"Thank you. Charity Shields. 42, Bopitts Lane. I've been taking care of my nephew for his parents. They've gone on holiday."

"Why did they choose you?"

"Probably because I was the last resort."

He didn't challenge her self-deprecation. "And why do you think he's been kidnapped?"

It was deep breath time. Telling bits of the story would make things even more complicated than a full account would. On the other hand …

"So you're implicating Mr McCarthy, successful farmer, member of the local history society, and staunch conservationist, of being involved in murder, attempted murder, and illegal business deals between PH Developments and the local council?"

"Yes."

He leaned forward, glancing right and left, in a theatrical display of speaking confidentially. "I should, er, keep those opinions to yourself. Otherwise, you might find yourself in court on a charge of slander. And you might find yourself very unpopular."

Charity widened her eyes. "Goodness. Lose my popularity? Over a murder, attempted murder, illegal dealings between a contractor and the local council, and a kidnapping. That certainly puts it into perspective. You're quite right. I need to rearrange my priorities."

"Finished?"

"No. I have the rest of my account."

"Make it as short as possible. I'm very busy."

"Doing what?"

"Just tell me what happened. Quickly."

"Do you mean gabble?"

"I mean keep it brief."

She gave him a brief account of her time as Caroline Holt.

The policeman almost looked pleased. "So, you presented yourself at PH Developments as someone, and something, that didn't exist, annoyed a senior member of staff, tried to gain access to confidential files, made your nephew spend whole days sitting in a store room, then left him at home to be kidnapped."

"I didn't leave him at home to be kidnapped. I left him at home for a couple of hours, and when I returned he'd been kidnapped. But I suppose your believing that he's been kidnapped is a small step forward."

"I didn't say I believed it. I was merely emphasising how ridiculous your entire story sounds, and pointing out to you that if he *has* been kidnapped, much of the blame will lie with you."

"So, what are you going to do?"

"Do? Well, we shall follow our customary missing persons procedure. If you find that he's returned home, please let us know immediately."

"And the rest of it?"

"Er, if we hear of anything suspicious, from another source, then we'll investigate. Good day, Miss Shields."

She turned away.

Then turned back.

"I told you that my nephew was put in a room upstairs, out of the way."

"Yes. What about it?"

"A few moments ago, you told me that I had made my nephew spend whole days sitting in a store room."

"Again, what about it?"

"I told you that he was in a room upstairs, out of the way. I didn't say that he was sitting in a store room."

"Well, in an office building, upstairs and out of the way generally means a store room."

"Oh. Happens a lot does it?"

"Good day, Miss Shields."

"Good day, Officer. You've been very helpful."

She made herself concentrate on the journey home. She was close to collapse. There was too much happening, too many people against her, and poor Eric missing.

As soon as she was home, she went straight to the kitchen and took out a bottle of wine. But she hesitated. She knew wine, and herself, well enough to know that one glass wouldn't be enough. She had her own rule about alcohol: not when she needed it. De-stress with a glass of wine, and soon it was two, three and … on and on. There was stress everywhere, and when you were fully in the de-stressing routine, soon you'd be looking for stress, just for the pleasure of relieving it.

She needed food, but she wasn't hungry.

She needed to think, but she no longer knew how.

She felt tears and sobs coming, and muttered, "I can't do this on my own."

A knock on the back door made her flinch. She was too vulnerable for a knock on any door, especially that one.

She called, "Who is it?"

The reply was a loud, urgent whisper.

"It's Suzy. Let me in."

CHAPTER TWENTY-SEVEN

The visitor had removed her long coat and dark glasses, but retained the headscarf. She accepted a mug of tea, relishing every sip.

Charity said, "I've been chasing a lot of loose ends. Are you going to join them up for me?"

"So far as background goes, I shall. But I've been keeping out of the way. I know some things, but I'll need you to tell me the details."

"Just before we set off on the background, and the fore-ground, how do you know who I am, where I live, what I've been doing?"

"I've been watching you. Following you."

"Since when?"

"Since you found Tom's body."

"Okay. Let's have the background."

"More tea, please."

As Charity waited for the water to boil again, she said, "Am I correct in assuming that you are Susan Frankland?"

"Yes."

"Am I also correct in assuming that Mr Orris is a bad guy?"

"Yes."

"The tea needs to stand, then cool. Do you want to make a start?"

"Yes. I'd better. There's a lot to cover, and we don't know how long we have."

"That sounds ominous."

"You've probably realised that we are dealing with ruthless, desperate people."

"Yes."

"It's a big step from crooked business deals to murder. That was a big mistake. Corruption is very difficult to establish, and very difficult to prove. We all know that when a council approves the building of hundreds of houses, there's corruption. We know it even when everyone connected with it, and thereby profiting from it, brings out the old cry of *Need more houses! Housing shortage! Housing crisis!* A succession of governments has ordered councils to meet targets for new houses. So the councils can say that the government told them to do it; and the contractors can say that the council told them to do it.

"So, the goverment *is* corrupt, but they *do* believe there is a housing crisis. They use doublethink. Or an easier version of it. They order the provision of independent statistics, having let it be known in advance what they want the statistics to prove. Of course the company which is going to provide the statistics will give the government what it wants."

Charity interrupted. "Suzy, this is interesting and disturbing, and I want to learn much more about it; and I want to bring down all these bad people; but my most pressing matter is the kidnapping of my nephew. Could I have the summary of what has happened, and we'll do the why it happened later?"

"Yes, you're right. The long explanations and analyses can follow. Right. Give me a few moments to arrange it in my head."

Charity placed the mugs on the table. Suzy sat looking at her tea, but didn't distract herself by drinking. Soon, she began to nod and move her right hand about as though conducting an internal symphony.

"Okay," she said abruptly. "Here goes. I work for the council, issuing, receiving and assessing tenders for various types of work. Councils are very keen advocates of outsourcing, paying other people to do the work, while also being very keen advocates of keeping a vast army of strimmers and mowers. Understandably, having established a system of paying other people to do the work, they are keen on deals which bring additional benefits, and additional kudos.

"So far, not necessarily justifiable, but understandable, especially when government requirements and legislation make demands. Houses must be built, facilities must be provided for the people who live in the houses, and health and safety legislation requires constant inspections and improvements. Now, at some point, the whole legally corrupt business of tendering can tip over into absolute illegal corruption. In simple terms, a contractor will pay for planning permission. The contractor might offer some facilities as a long-term plan, but money will be paid for permission to build. The corrupt council official then pulls out the government instructions about the building of houses, and claims official approval. An artificial tendering process could be used, but word goes round: don't bother with the expense of tendering because the decision has already been made."

Charity said, "Suzy, you're doing it again. I know it's important background, and I am very keen to investigate and bring bad people to justice, but before all that, I am anxious to rescue a kidnapped child."

"I'm not sure the objectives can be separated, but I understand your point. Right. Tom Henry had been involved in some small contracts with the council which would not have borne close scrutiny, but which weren't big enough to draw attention. Politicians and the police are interested only when something might be exposed and lead to embarrassment. That, above all, is what they can't bear, can't tolerate. And that is when all those involved in dishonest dealings move away from one another, proclaim their innocence and blame everyone else."

"So what happened with Tom?" Charity asked, keen to keep it moving along.

"Tom found out about a secret deal."

"The houses on McCarthy's land."

"Yes."

"How did Tom find out?"

"I told him."

"You told him?"

"Not directly. I found out about the proposal accidentally. The old case of seeing something that I wasn't meant to see. On Orris's desk. From then on, I tried to find out more, but there was nothing anywhere in writing. ("Snap," said Charity.) What I did find, through persistence, was one of those obscure study reports which use hundreds of words to say nothing. At least, it said things whose meaning could be understood only afterwards. It would say something like 'consideration of utilisation of agricultural zone within the dotted red line to be earmarked for possible use for the benefit of a growing and diversifying local community."

"Which with the benefit of what you had seen before translated to 'build several hundred houses on two sheep fields.'"

"Yes. Now back to Tom. His firm being only a moderately successful performer, with no power to exert, no powerful connections, he steadily developed as an enquirer. By that I mean always asking for news, possible openings. He had his marketing manager, but he liked to do things on his own initiative. He liked to take me to lunch. In return, I gave him advance notification of jobs that might be requiring tenders, and let him know very vaguely what sort of things the council might be looking at in the future. It was harmless stuff, and I thought of it as giving a helping hand to a relatively small contractor.

"With the knowledge which I now had, small gestures, nods and winks, as it were, started to seem like coded messages, and I began to unravel bits of the code. Not very difficult. When I heard Orris mention 'the Agland Venture' to someone, I understood. I also began to compile a list of those who were involved.

"The next breakthrough came when the contractor rang and I took the call. Contractors can be as careful and secretive as the KGB for ninety per cent of the time; but for the other ten percent, they are the world's biggest tactless blunderers. By the time that the call was cut off, about three seconds, I knew that the selected contractor was Hendersons. They provide the full package. They *own* companies which provide building materials, they own architects and surveyors, they own transport companies, and they own health and safety consultants and legal advisers. Tom could never compete with them. At that point, I decided to stir things up a bit. I dropped a big hint to Tom. I told him that I had nothing for him, that it wasn't fair to keep asking me, because I wouldn't tell him even if I knew about a big contract for building houses on nearby agricultural land. I asked him did he understand. He said, 'Yes', and I said, 'Good'. I looked at my watch, and said that I must be going back to the office."

Suzy sighed and made a wry face. "I didn't know that Tom would react as forcefully as he did. He demanded a meeting with Orris, and, probably as it became more heated, with Tom becoming more frustrated and Orris more arrogant, he accused Orris of malpractices and threatened to reveal. What he *should* have done, if anything, was to suggest that it might be to everyone's advantage if he were to be given a slice of the cake. Orris could have discussed it with Hendersons, and they would probably have let him have a small sub-contract to keep him quiet."

"Did they link you with the information?"

"I think it occurred when I heard Orris mutter to Bagnall, one of the bad guys, that mumble, mumble would have to be dealt with. At that moment, Orris turned and looked at me. I looked back, not knowing whether it was worse to hold the look or to look away. But in that moment, he *knew*, and I knew that he knew, and so on. From that point, in meetings and in conversations, I began to recognise coded messages, about *me*. Nothing overt, of course, mentions of staffing reviews, unreliability in certain areas, necessary measures. That last one seemed menacing.

"I made an appointment with Tom. I started to tell him

to step back, but he interrupted me to tell me that he was going to have a meeting with one of the main players, tap of the nose, at a certain time, near this person's house. When I asked who it was, he hushed me. When I asked were they going to meet in one of the sheep fields, he chuckled and said, 'Not quite'. Guessing where it would be, I said nothing. I suggested that he take Bernie along, but he made a little hand gesture. He wanted to do it by himself."

"Well," said Charity, "he did that. Although Bernie nearly followed him soon after."

"Yes. I liked Tom, but he was a silly man."

"What about the affair with Bernie's wife?"

"Probably, Bernie's interpretation of Tom's secretive ways. Great partnership."

"Sorry: I interrupted."

"I'll willingly be brief now. I'm fed up of talking. Conciseness. I went to the wood, and waited in a fairly central place. I heard them talking, briefly, then a gasp and a wail from Tom. I crept forward very slowly, until I could see McCarthy, bent over Tom's body. Now, for my lucky moment: I stood on a dry branch. McCarthy would have plunged into the wood, but at the same moment, you and Eric came chattering along. Moving the body was too complicated and difficult in seconds, so he went off and hid. When you found the body, you conducted your little investigation, until it occurred to you that the murderer might still be there. You saw him. You ran. He ran. I ran, ready to assist, but he saw me and came after me instead. He didn't catch me. I rang in with a made-up illness, and since then, I've been watching *you* and evading *them*. And now it's your turn."

With no need for background to slow her down,

Charity rushed through her account. At the end, Suzy said, "Our accounts connect very well, except that you have an extra character, about whom I know nothing."

"Marie Ridings. Well, let's leave her on one side for the present. We have her background, and all the motives. I have some more questions, but they can wait. My priority is Eric. Why have they taken him? Not for ransom. Not for my promise to be silent, because I could ignore any promises when I had Eric back. That leaves a trap."

"I think you're right."

"So, to rescue Eric, I must go into that trap."

"Right again."

"Not a happy prospect. I haven't done well on my own so far."

"Leaving aside my disagreement with your performance, you won't be on your own. You'll have me."

She grinned. "They don't stand a chance."

CHAPTER TWENTY-EIGHT

"Right," Charity said, "the plan has been agreed. Bernie's drooping mouth indicates a lack of enthusiasm, but he's in the team, and the only way out is by being a coward and a traitor."

Bernie said. "I'm neither of those. Reluctant and apprehensive, yes; coward and a traitor, no."

He'd been invited to Charity's house for an early evening drink and a strategy review. It wasn't a lie, just not what he was expecting.

Suzy said, "Let's do a little rehearsal. I'll be Ms Ridings."

"Very well. Which it isn't."

"Go on, then. Tell me what you want."

Bernie inflated, then released it and subsided. Again, the chest expanded. "Marie, I want access to the confidential files. I need a copy of the key to the room, and to the filing cabinet."

"Bernie, even Tom didn't ask for that. He was quite happy to leave me in full control of those files which you and he don't even need to see."

Bernie said gloomily, "You sound just like her."

"Stay in character, Bernie."

"Marie, in the absence of Mr Henry, I am the owner of this company. It's absurd that I should be denied access by a member of my staff to the files which *I own*. And as the owner, I do not want anything to be inaccessible to me. I am the one who is ultimately responsible."

"Bernie, just tell me which file you want, and I'll provide it for you."

"All of them! All the … files. And I don't want them delivered. I want access to them. Now!"

"I shall have to arrange for copies of the keys to be made."

"Don't bother. Give me yours."

"But I need access to those files."

"When you need one, come to me and ask."

Charity gave him the finger and thumb of approval. Suzy nodded, but stayed in character.

"Now!" Bernie repeated. "The keys!"

"I'll have to sort things out first."

"Now! Give me the keys or you're sacked."

"No!"

"In that case, I shall ring the police and have the keys removed from you, and you removed from the building."

Suzy wasn't done. She leaned forward and said, "You don't want to do that, Bernie. You *really* don't want to do that. I know a lot of things about this company that would put you in a lot of trouble with the police. I'm talking about prison, Bernie. You and Tom. You were the ones who signed everything that's in those confidential files."

Charity said, "Take your time, Bernie. Think about what she said, and use it against her."

Bernie clicked his fingers. "Are you saying that you knew the company was in breach of the regulations, even acting illegally, and instead of doing the right thing, you obtained our signatures? That makes you more than an accessory: it puts you in charge of the malpractices. I think I'd better call the police anyway. Just let me have those keys, and I'll find out what's been going on."

"No."

"You leave me no choice."

"Have the police number ready, Bernie. No empty bluffs. Especially in view of what I might do next."

She stood and ran up the stairs, calling, "What's next, Bernie? Think."

He shrugged. "Run after you and grab you?"

She came back down the stairs. "There's an obvious problem with that."

"The only way," said Charity, "is to go upstairs before she does and stand guard while calling the police and reporting your suspicion of illegalities in your company. Ask for both male and female officers. Then, she will have the choice of letting you have the keys or letting the police have them."

"But tell her what you are about to do. It's in your interest to give her one last chance."

Bernie phewed for all of them. Suzy reassured him with, "That brilliant performance might not be needed, Bernie, but I think we all expect a lot of resistance, so at least we've anticipated all the obstacles. You were very impressive when you were roused out of your reluctance. Stick to it."

"Thanks, Bernie," Charity said. "You're now free to leave and go and have your tea. Suzy and I are going to go on with our side of things."

"I'm happy to stay if you need me. I don't like to leave you both to … to ….I'll let you know how it goes tomorrow. Shall we meet here again?"

"Unless there's a crisis. For example if it does come to your calling the police, and they say they're very busy, and they'll try to visit next Wednesday, something like that, then call us and we'll come running."

As Charity took him to the door, she said, "The only thing you did wrong in the rehearsal was having to build up to taking control. Do that from the start. She might respond in different ways; stick to the script. Don't allow digressions."

As he walked away, he looked as though he was shedding all the resolve and good advice. She called, "Marketing Manager, Bernie! And she's just a disobedient member of staff."

He tried to look determined and confident, but she preferred his earlier performance, when he became frustrated and angry.

When she went back, Suzy said, "It's nearly time to go."

"Are you sure about this?"

"It's your plan."

"But I've given myself the easy task, and yours is the difficult and dangerous one."

"If I can't find a way in, or the dogs are in ferocious mode, I might not be doing anything."

"And if he doesn't attend, there's no Plan B. There can't be. We need him to be there."

Shortly after, they slipped out of the back door. Suzy had parked a little way off, so Charity reversed onto the road and waited for her. Cars were needed tonight, in case there was a crisis. The usual contingency.

They both parked in the car park, but well away from each other. Charity was hoping that after the assumed reports from Orris and Ms Ridings, McCarthy would be keen to bolster his reputation by attending the local history society meeting. An accumulation of alibis was better than one at the end.

"You big poser," she muttered when she saw his green Defender turn into the car park. But she was pleased to see him. As she watched him go into the building, she felt relief mixed with apprehension. "Well, this is it," she said. "This is the plan which we agreed."

She stepped out of her car, ready to give the thumbs-up for Suzy, but smiled as Suzy drove past, waving from her window.

Inside, they were settling into their seats, some people looking at Suzy with the pleasure that society members feel when someone comes back for more. But they were all aglow in the presence of the great man. He had a large plaster on his forehead, and there were signs of some bruising. Even more intense simpering sycophancy was the order of the evening. McCarthy acknowledged it all with smoothly polished modesty.

"Well, I must say," Len Brent said," that after your nasty accident, it's very good of you to turn up tonight."

McCarthy dismissed the compliment with a modest wave. "If local historians aren't dogged and determined, what hope is there?"

There were approving murmurs and chuckles. Charity did her best to join in.

In normal circumstances, Charity would have found the first topic very interesting. It was about local home industries long ago. The second one had some interest, too, being about the effects of the Enclosures Acts. But her mind kept wandering, and she kept trying to avoid looking at McCarthy, in case he recognised her.

It was near the end of the second topic that she carelessly glanced in his direction, at the precise moment that he did the same. She quickly looked about at the other members, but a half-glance back showed that he was still looking at her, thinking .... remembering ... thinking. Then, she saw in his eyes, not only recognition, but the strong suspicion about what her presence, and his own presence, might mean.

"I'm sorry, guys," he said, standing up and putting on his jacket. "I'm afraid my headaches have returned. Overdone it. Very unfortunate. I was enjoying this very much. But will you please excuse me?"

Apart from Charity, there was a unanimous chorus of reassurances for the great man.

Having turned her telephone to silent, she had left it on, ready to send the warning message to Suzy.

The message wouldn't go. Something was blocking it.

She rose and said, "Sorry. So sorry. I must go, too."

She hesitated for a few moments inside the door, as the Defender roared out the car park. He was talking on his telephone.

His worked, but *hers* didn't.

She dashed to her car, trying the telephone again. It wouldn't send a message, and there was no answer when she rang.

She drove out onto the main road, and set off in pursuit.

CHAPTER TWENTY-NINE

Charity was being decisive while being the most indecisive that she'd ever been. She was trying to avoid being seen by McCarthy while wanting to go past him and arrive at the farm in time to warn Suzy. It was no good. Calm thought was needed. Realism. She couldn't go past him, arrive at the farm ahead of him, and in time to warn Suzy, and for Suzy to have time to leave the house, and *then* for both of them to turn in the narrow lane and depart; all without being stopped or at least clearly seen by McCarthy. She would stay close to McCarthy and follow him to the farm, ready to help Suzy if ...if what? She didn't want to think about that.

It wasn't a long or complicated journey, and there wasn't a lot of traffic. He must have seen her. But now he knew that he would have to deal with two people, She reached down to the heavy spanner which she kept in the car, just in case. She had never even thought about *how* she would ever use it. Self-defence videos were all about fast and supple martial arts techniques, not instruction on how to wield your spanner.

As they turned into the lane to the farm, she became aware that he wasn't driving quickly; not dawdling, just driving in a slow, careful way.

As they approached the farm, she understood. Head-lamps appeared behind her. When he'd used his telephone, he'd called for assistance, and she knew what was going to happen.

Just before the farm, the Defender stopped, and the lights were switched off. The same thing happened behind her. She was trapped. For a moment, she thought of locking the doors, cowering, hoping, waiting for it to be over.

No! She had come to help Suzy, and she was going to do it. She opened her door.

McCarthy called, "You take care of that one. I'll see to the other one."

"No problem," Marie replied, striding forward.

For distraction, Charity pushed her door fully open. As Marie stepped aside, Charity took one step and swung the spanner over and down onto her shoulder. As she staggered, Charity did the same to the other shoulder. Marie merely gasped twice, and sank to her knees, groaning. Charity longed to do some more swinging, just to be sure. But that wasn't her way. Besides, she might be needed urgently. Suzy's car was still here. So, then, was Suzy. Perhaps.

She left Marie panting on her knees, and ran to the front door of the farm. It was closed, and locked. He didn't want Suzy to slip out that way. She ran round to the back. That door was locked, too. She thought of calling the police, but what would they find? A woman who had been attacked with a spanner, and McCarthy trying to arrest someone who had broken into his house. The circumstances were all wrong for trying to convince the police. But as a last resort to prevent the murder of Suzy, and herself.

That wasn't a remote possibility. They had joined that elite group of endangered humans who *knew too much*.

As she felt the back window, lights were being turned on, She ducked down and crawled away as the kitchen light was turned on. She went back to the front of the house. Again, the windows were shut tight, and she had to duck down as the front room light was switched on. In the light that was shone on the ground, she could see the dark shape of McCarthy as he moved about the room. When the dark shape disappeared, she slowly rose and peeped through the window. He'd gone, but to where? And where was Suzy?

The second question was suddenly answered.

Above her was a rustle. She looked up and saw an open window, and another dark shape. But this one was was slithering down a drainpipe. It wasn't a smooth descent, but it was fast, ending with a small thud as Suzy landed.

"How traditional," Charity said.

"Can't beat the old ways. Let's go."

As Suzy reached her car, she said, "Leave your door open until you start your engine. No advance noises."

Charity glanced up and saw McCarthy at the bedroom window, then not there as he moved quickly. "Too late!" she called, running to her car. With perfect synchronisation, they started their engines, spun their cars round in three-point turns as McCarthy hurtled out of the front door, and they roared off down the lane.

Charity started to brake when she saw Marie, her arms

folded across her chest to hold her shoulders, standing in her path, looking determined to stand her ground. But as soon as she started to slow, Charity knew she must call Marie's bluff, and increased her speed. She did swerve slightly, but Marie had already leapt aside, her back against her own car.

It was dark, but Charity was in the mood for taking risks with her speed. But when they were out of the lane, she slowed as Suzy flashed her. She saw the small factory and turned into the parking area. Suzy followed and parked beside her. They turned off their lights and waited.

Not for long. McCarthy's vehicle hurtled by, closely followed by Marie's car. Charity was both relieved and disappointed to see her driving after the shoulder blows. She didn't want to break anything, but she didn't want her opponent to be quite so up and about, so soon.

When Suzy walked round to her car, Charity said, "The full story shortly. Did you find anything?"

"Not much. By the time I'd climbed in and made friends with the dogs, there were only a few minutes before he came tearing up and I had to retreat. And almost everything is on people's computers now. Except when they take information by telephone. I found a scribbled note of Orris's address. Your boy might be there."

"But if they've set a trap, why not include the farm? He was in a big panic when it suddenly occurred to him that you might be there."

"They might have thought it was too obvious."

"But they must have known that I didn't know the other addresses."

"True. Perhaps it isn't a trap."

"That's good and bad news. "What *is* their purpose?"

Suzy did a big shrug. "I don't know. With all the official corruption supporting them, I don't know why they thought they needed to do it. Another thing: why should seeing you at the meeting suggest that I was at his house? If someone had been watching you, and me, he wouldn't have taken so long to recognise you."

"It might have been a variation of the panic that we all have when we go somewhere and don't remember locking the door."

"Perhaps. By the way, assuming that they've gone round to your place, did you lock the doors?"

She smiled. "I think so. But if they're determined, or desperate, enough, they'll find a way in."

"True. So, what's your suggestion?"

Charity thought for a moment and said, "Two of us, two of them. Back to my place, and let's turn the tables. Which one do you want to follow?"

"Ooh, choices. Which one, which one? I can't. You choose. It's your inspired idea."

"Which might lead to another crisis. Okay, you follow McCarthy. But he might just go back to the farm, in which case, call me, and I'll tell you where I am."

"Right. Let's do it before we meet them coming back. And remember, we aren't experts at this, so circumspection all the way. Better to lose them than be caught."

"Follow me. There's a communal parking area at the end of the road next to mine. Tenby Road. We can wait in there."

They drove stealthily out of the car park, hesitating at the entrance before committing themselves. Then they drove quickly to Charity's road, where they settled in the darkest corner of the small parking area. Leaving their cars, with Charity leading, they went along a narrow passage between houses, and stopped where it joined Charity's road.

Charity peeped round and said, "No cars outside, but of course plenty parked along the street. If I were in their position, I'd park out of sight, but where I could see, and wait for me to arrive home."

"Is the road open at the other end?"

"No, it stops, and there's another little passage joining it to the other end of Tenby Road. We could go along this road and look round the corner."

"We're lucky they didn't pick this spot."

"Yes. Unless we're walking into another trap."

"We haven't had the first one yet."

"So far as we know. We might be following steps into the trap."

They hurried along to the end of Tenby Road, walked very slowly along the passage, and looked. They both drew back immediately. The Defender was on this side of the road, a few feet away. Across the road was Marie's car, and they could see her in the front seat, staring intently ahead.

"Just as well she's concentrating," Suzy whispered.

"If she's on look-out duty, that must mean he's in my house. Bugs, bombs, or just waiting to kill me when I walk in."

"Or just snooping. But you're probably right. One of what you suggested."

"Horrible thought. But there's one good thing about it. We're ahead of them, and that in itself suggests very strongly that they are pretty dim."

She took a few paces back, tapping at her telephone,

now working perfectly. "Hi, Bernie. Sorry to bother you. Do you know Marie's addresss? No, nothing to be nervous about, Bernie. We just want to have a look from the outside. Bernie! McCarthy is in my house, and Marie is being look-out. Yes. That's good. Very sensible. Very useful. No, I'll wait. I don't want you to call back."

She looked at Suzy and said, "Thank employee welfare requirements. I was counting on something of the sort. Hi, Bernie. Yes. Right, that's great. No, nothing risky. Just a bit of observation. You have a good sleep, ready for your role in the morning. Your vital role, Bernie. Okay. Goodnight."

"So," Suzy said. "We have three addresses. That might be a winning hand."

She became alert as they heard footsteps. They pressed themselves against the wall of the last house. The door of the Defender opened and closed, and the engine rumbled.

"Come on!" Charity pulled Suzy's sleeve, and started to move away. Suzy pulled back. "Charity. We have their addresses. We don't need to pursue, risking being seen."

"Good point. Let's saunter back to our cars, and think about new choices. We're not going to follow anyone, so I suggest that our choice is now Marie or Orris."

"I'm not sure of the relevance, but I've worked with Orris, and you've worked with Marie ..."

"Then let's switch. Unless the rogues have our photographs on a rogues gallery, Orris doesn't know what I look like, and Marie doesn't know what you look like. If one of us is seen, that might provide valuable time for escape."

"Good thinking, Charity. Right, then. Back here in two hours?"

"Unless ..."

"If 'unless' happens, we meet back here sooner, and agree a plan. And we do it together. No going it alone. Agreed?"

"Of course."

"With you, there's no 'of course'. Just stick to the plan."

CHAPTER THIRTY

Charity's usual driving method was to avoid hitting, and being hit by, other cars. Not tonight. She barely noticed other cars as she concentrated on following the GPS instructions. Her current one was very bossy with not a trace of charm, and that suited the present purpose. Charity wanted to be told, firmly and clearly, exactly where to go. It worked perfectly, although the GPS couldn't understand why she wanted to stop at the end of the road; the mechanical lady wanted Charity to finish the task by going all the way to the door. Charity pointlessly explained to her and switched it off.

Marie lived in a row of old, tall houses, the sort that excite estate agents. Opposite the house were trees and a small park. A walking and thinking sort of park, not one with multicoloured activities for children. Charity could imagine Marie walking there, thinking about illegal deals and the disposal of difficult people.

The word 'premeditated' entered Charity's head as she stuffed the spanner as far as it would go into her jacket pocket. The law didn't accept her need for self-defence weapons. It might accept the presence of a spanner in her car because it was a tool, and people keep tools in cars; but it wouldn't accept her need to take it to the house of an enemy. She was expected to wait for a few hours for the police to intervene.

Number 19 was dark, and there was no car in the drive or on the road. Marie set off before Charity did, and knew her way home. Had she gone to McCarthy's place? Or for a drink in a pub? Well, conjecturing wasn't going to help. She went along the narrow passage between the wall of the house and the high wall which kept the neighbours away. At the back, the house looked very gloomy and forbidding. It seemed a suitable house for plotting, manipulating Marie.

There was a garden, looking more like an impenetrable jungle. Not even an interesting one, just a chaos of brambles and nettles, so far as she could see. Certainly not a good route for an escape.

It also looked like a suitable house for keeping a prisoner. There must be a lot of rooms, with thick walls. She felt a spasm of dread as she thought of poor Eric, a prisoner, in the darkness, alone and afraid. She walked carefully over the narrow patio, and, not ruling anything out, she tried the handle of the back door. As she expected, it was locked. Farther along, there were was a French window. She decided to try that, too.

It opened.

She felt a prickle of alarm. Why was it open? People do forget opening French windows earlier, not concentrating as they go out of the front and back doors. But not Marie people.

She could almost feel Marie watching her, an arrogant smile on her face, drawing Charity into her web.

Eric! That was all that mattered. She must take risks for his sake.

She slipped through the narrow gap and closed the door.

Now what? A large old house, in almost complete darkness. She needed a bit of light but that was beyond daring. She must feel her way very slowly and carefully all the way, through rooms, corridors and up stairs, perhaps even into an attic.

And Marie, and perhaps McCarthy, might arrive very soon.

She hated this darkness, this dark and vast house. This was like being blind. All she could do was grope, arms stretched out, her feet taking tiny steps.

But how long would this take?

She needed light.

She had light.

McCarthy spoke first. "You really are stupid. Obviously, it was a trap."

Then, Marie, standing beside him. "You're right out of your depth, Charity. You always have been. Caroline Holt. Oh, really. Come on, now. How thick do you think we are?"

"Extremely," Charity replied. "Of course I suspected a trap. But it wouldn't take a genius to know that anyone with a trace of decency would accept the risk."

Marie sniffed. "Ah, well I don't have any patience with decency. I'm a businesswoman. Much more important things to think about."

"Is Eric here?"

McCarthy grinned. "He might be."

"If you've harmed him …"

"What, Charity? What will you do?" He oozed contempt. "You must know how high the stakes are. You must know that you are our sole danger, and must be disposed of."

He watched her, reading her simple thought. He wrinkled his nose and shook his head. "Oh, you're thinking about your new friend, aren't you? Well, she's gone to the other part of the trap. She'll be dealt with in the same way. Now, I'm not going to do that long speech thing that they do in the films and books, while you devise a means of escape. There's no escape."

"So, I'm hopelessly trapped."

"Yes. Exactly so."

Charity gave a lip shrug. "Well, what are we waiting for? Let's do this thing."

This time, Marie responded. "Oh, we shall. Don't even think about trying to use the spanner in your pocket. So typical of you. I think what I hate most about you is your damn delusion of superiority. You see us as an office administrator and a farmer. You've been out-thought and out-manoeuvred all the way, and you're about to be killed, but you still think that there must be a way out of this problem because you're too clever to be killed by a couple of common criminals."

McCarthy pulled out a gun. He smiled as he saw Charity's response. "My intention was to use the knife. This thing is so damn noisy."

Marie burst forward. Three quick strides, and she swung the hammer, with no backlift, straight at Charity's head. Charity raised her arm and took the blow on it. The pain of the breaking bone merely provided the fuel for her own swing with the spanner, smashing Marie's cheekbone.

Marie yelped and staggered, then yelped again, as the bullet hit her.

"You cretin!" she bellowed, dropping to the floor.

"Sorry," McCarthy called cheerfully. "I shan't miss this time."

The lounge door crashed open. McCarthy turned, his gun pointing at Suzy. Charity hurtled forward and struck him on the head with the spanner. He bellowed and fired. Charity hit him again, and he sank to his knees. This time, she struck the wrist of the gun hand. And for good measure, she practised the shoulder strike again. There was another cry of pain.

"Better," Charity said, picking up the gun. "Definitely better. I just need more practice on my swing."

She looked gratefully at Suzy. "Why?"

"I decided it was probably a trap. Even two traps."

"Well done. We'll go into it later. Please do a quick search for Eric while I watch these two."

McCarthy twisted into a sitting position. He sounded drunk as he said, "I think we need to discuss a deal for the benefit of all of us."

Charity laughed. "You look and sound ridiculous. You are beaten, your illegal business is destroyed, and you think you're in a position to do a deal."

"We have something you want very much. Someone, I should say."

Marie gasped, "And in the event of anything happening to us, bits of your boy will be removed."

"So you anticipated failure, did you?"

McCarthy said, "Always have a Plan B."

"What? Keep killing people? That's your Plan B?"

"No. Those were just necessary measures because people kept interfering with the plans. The current Plan B is to make you understand that your boy will be severely harmed unless you cooperate."

"Right. So, I cooperate, my boy is returned, what, then?"

"That's entirely up to you. Your sentence has been deferred. Be in our way again, and you'll be killed."

Suzy returned and said, "I can't see him anywhere. That leaves Orris."

Charity smiled. "I think it leaves someone else. Address or pain, Marie. Your choice."

CHAPTER THIRTY-ONE

They hadn't driven far when they heard the sirens. When she called the police, Charity used the magic word 'shooting'. That instantly stirred them into action. Now, she was dashing, with Suzy right behind her, because the police would soon be chasing *her*. Even without the corruption in at least one member of the force, the response was easy to predict. A highly-respected local man, and an assistant, victims of a brutal attack, by that annoying woman. And someone else was in danger now. They must stop her and her accomplice before someone else was harmed. That's how it would go.

There was so much happening, so many things that could happen; but Charity made herself keep her mind firmly focused on one thing: the rescue of Eric. Soon, the sirens would be following her. It didn't matter. Eric was all that mattered.

They couldn't do the usual thing of parking at the end of the road, because the cottage that they wanted was in a neglected little lane in an even older part of the town. They

parked a short way away. It didn't matter much because
Charity wasn't going to be cautious and careful.

Seeing a window to one side of the door, she put Suzy
between the window and the door, and bent her legs a little.
As expected, when she knocked, someone peeped through
the curtains.

Suzy called, "Police! Open up."

The door was opened, and the voice said, "I haven't
done anything wrong."

From within the house, a familiar voice called, "Hi,
Charity. I've been expecting you. Come on in."

"Thank you, Eric. I'm glad you had confidence in me,
and you're commendably polite, but at fault on one thing.
It isn't your house. It's this lady's."

"Come in."

They walked though the short hall and turned left into a
small and cosy room. Eric sat in an armchair, his iPad in his
hands. He looked up mischievously.

"Eric," said Charity. "How are you?"

"Fine," he replied. "But I think I'm ready to come
home."

Charity turned and said, "Is that okay with you, Linda?"

"Of course. But I shall miss him. He's such a lovely
boy."

"Eric," Charity said, "have you been pretending to be a
lovely boy?"

"Pre*ten*ding?" Eric replied.

"Come on. Let's take you home. Thank you for looking
after him, Linda."

They all heard the sirens. Linda said, "Oh, dear, I
suppose I'll go to prison."

Charity shook her head. "Let's see what a muddle

they're going to make of this. I suggest you open the door before they knock it down."

She did, and moments later three policeman clumped and clattered into the small room, making it seem very much smaller. One thrust himself forward and said, "Charity Shields? Susan Frankland? I'm arresting you on suspicion of causing grievous bodily harm. You do not have to say anything, but it may harm your defence if you do not mention, when questioned, something which you later rely on in court. Anything you do say may be given in evidence."

"It's what I expected. You've made a complete mess of it. You may certainly write my comments, and I shall use them later to cause you great embarrassment. Why have you not arrested those two villains?"

"Mr McCarthy and Ms Ridings are currently receiving medical attention following your attack."

"Wrong word. Defence. Not attack."

"I understand that you are armed."

"Ah, yes. My spanner. And, oh, lord. I forgot about that. McCarthy's gun. Don't panic. I'm about to take the gun out."

They panicked, bristling with a mixed desire to engage in a shoot-out and to duck. She said, "I'll do it as they used to do in the cowboy films, finger and thumb. Oh. Typical. It doesn't want to come out. Here, you do it."

She offered her left hip to him. He came forward cautiously and removed the gun.. She said, "You'll find that two bullets have been fired. One by Mr McCarthy into Ms Ridings, although I think that was an accident."

"An accident?"

"Yes. He was trying to kill me. The other shot was fired,

by him again, at my colleague. The bullet is probably in the wall next to the door. So, that's two attempted murders by Mr McCarthy."

"Yes, well, that will all be part of our investigation. In the meantime, you are both required to accompany me to the police station. You will then meet with a custody sergeant. I shall go over the background, time, necessity and reason for arrest. The sergeant will go over welfare questions with you both. He will then authorise detention, and you will each be taken to a cell.

"Oh, Eric! I'm so sorry about this. Linda, I'd ask you to mind him, but you're rather involved with these bad people, aren't you? All they have to do is take him off you again. I must ask for police protection."

The policeman's head was spinning. He tried the simple method of asking Eric. "Why are you here?"

"I was kidnapped," was the equally simple reply.

"Has she told you what to say?"

"She's a cat's mother. Do you mean Charity?"

"Yes."

"No. Of course not. Are you calling me a liar?"

"Just answer my questions."

"I did."

"I shall arrange for a special officer to come and take care of you. In the meantime, I trust this lady won't have any objection to taking care of you for a little longer."

"I've no objection."

Eric shook his head. "It isn't safe. The bad people will come back. I'll stay with Charity."

"You can't. She is being arrested."

"Arrest me, then."

"You haven't done anything wrong."

Eric leapt up, ran at him and kicked his leg. "Now, I have. Arrest me."

The policeman winced. Charity laughed. "All that armour, but no protection against a little boy's kick."

"Right! Out! Now!"

"Oh, dear," Suzy said. "You've really upset him."

"*I* didn't kick him. They should be arresting the boy."

"You mean they've done it wrong a*gain*?"

"Cut it out," the policeman growled.

"Charity!"

"I'm sorry, Eric. Hopefully, this special officer will arrive soon. But I suppose the bad people would be stupid to kidnap you again. It wouldn't be in keeping with their pretence of respectability."

She looked at Linda. "As for you, don't pretend to me, to him or to yourself that you care about him. You care only about your self-pitying self."

"Come on," said the policeman, taking hold of her arm, and leading her to the front door.

"Wait!"

Linda stood in the hall, looking very small and lonely. Charity looked at her intensely, encouraging her.

"Eric *was* kidnapped. McCarthy and ... Ms Ridings ... and a man at the council are criminals." She looked at Charity, and with a sad smile said, "You see, I *have* read Confidential File PH/TH/422."

CHAPTER THIRTY-TWO

"Fear of embarrassment," said Suzy. "Where law and order, social stability, morals and ethics all fail, fear of embarrassment will always move mountains.

"Even moving some powerful people in high places. I expect that the matter had to go to some high place before the investigation and arrests were approved."

"The people have been removed, for a while, but the system is still there. Other people will fill the gaps. And in a little while, the big four will reappear in different roles. Soft arrests, soft punishments, soft returns."

"Murder, attempted murders, kidnap and various forms of fraud? At least McCarthy should have a long sentence."

"He will. But long sentences have a strange way of becoming short ones."

"And the people who did the kidnapping continue to be not named."

Bernie sighed, yet again. "So, Tom is in the concrete base of the new post office building."

"There's a certain aptness about it, isn't there?" Charity said. "Builder buried in a building."

The gallows humour failed. Bernie wasn't to be cheered up. Charity tried again. "And Marie's gone."

"I know she was somewhat overbearing, but she was efficient. Running the place without her is going to be difficult."

"I nominate Suzy."

"What?"

"What?"

"Do you want to go back to working at the council?"

"No."

"Right, then. Bernie needs someone bright, with lots of character, and, as he will now be the target for the shady dealers, he needs someone to help him to keep the company above board."

Bernie sniffed. "So instead of having a criminal running me, I'll have an amateur detective running me."

"Working with you, Bernie." She looked at Suzy. "Of course, she might not want to."

Suzy thought about it. "It has a certain appeal. But it's up to Bernie. He owns the company."

At last, he smiled. "Yes. It suits me very well. Especially as it will release me from all that selection business."

"And *you*," Suzy said, "will continue to be a lady of leisure."

"I'm not sure for how much longer. Strict frugality is required, and I'm not very good at it. Especially since Eric took me back into unhealthy eating and drinking. And he's been a big drain on my financial resources. Fortunately, he will be reclaimed tomorrow."

Eric looked up from his book. "So you want me to go?"

"No. I meant fortunately for my financial resources. I'd be very happy to keep you. Until adolescence, when you will change into something horrible. They all do. At that point, I'd happily sell you to the highest bidder. But until then, I hope you will visit me often because you brighten my life."

Eric, grunted, frowned and hid behind his book.

"Did the police ever apologise?" Suzy asked.

"Yes and no. They sent me a long letter which was entirely in councilspeak, in which they acknowledged my contribution to their very effective investigation."

From behind the book, Eric said, "Sherlock Holmes had the same problem."

"That's right, Eric. Well observed. They also mentioned in an obscure way that their rotten apple will be dealt with appropriately. As for the rest, I suppose it's the old one about having what you pay for. If you keep reducing numbers, and reducing what those numbers may do without the danger of complaints from the public, then you reduce the quality."

"And sniffing for danger, asking people what they're doing and what's in the bag, are called harassment."

"Exactly."

Bernie said, "What about Linda?"

"On that particular matter," Charity said, "we were in perfect harmony with the police. She had been asked to take care of a boy, and she took very good care of him. Eric has willingly confirmed that. I think the expression is least said, soonest mended. And it was because of her accumulated knowledge, and late willingness to reveal it, that we were able to move to a rapid conclusion, which didn't include the great inconvenience of a spell in prison for Suzy and me.

"And," she added, "I suspect that the loss of Linda would have had a greater effect on your company than the loss of Marie. Marie was very curious and observant. But please give Linda a title to reflect the work that she does."

"With the added interest of my new role," said Suzy, "did the the police go through all the confidential files?"

Bernie smiled. "They started to. After the first few files, there were some gasps and groans, an inspector was called in, *he* gasped and groaned, and the files were put back in the cabinet. When he gave me the key, the inspector said, "Be careful in future.""

"They didn't want to kick the ants' nest."

"Yes. Wrong, but understandable. And for an entirely selfish motive, I'm glad."

"Any sign of progress with …?"

"No. I suppose I'm pleased that she wasn't having an affair with Tom, but in a way it's even harder on the ego to know that she didn't leave me for someone else, she just didn't want to be with me. I can see very clearly now that it had been developing for a long time. She didn't respect me."

"Put it behind you, Bernie. You're a good fellow with lots of hidden strengths."

"Well-hidden. I certainly can't find them. But thank you."

"You didn't even have your big showdown with Marie."

"No. I'll never know how it would have gone."

"Bernie," Suzy said earnestly. "There are plenty of other Maries in the world. They just look different. Contractors, council officials, taxmen, shopkeepers, bus drivers, people in pubs. They don't want you to be assertive. That's why you must be. You must be the Marketing Manager all the time, with everyone. Sad, but true."

"Well, quite," Suzy said. "But it's time for a fresh start, eh, Bernie?"

"Yes," he said with some determination. "Yes, it is."

———

Angie and Carl arrived the next day, brown and refreshed. Charity played her part as well as she could. "Oh, we had a quiet time, but I don't think Eric was very bored. Were you, Eric?"

In character, he said, "Nah, it wasn't so bad."

"His clothes have been washed. There are a few additional items which I bought."

"Oh, that's fine."

Carl said, "What's that, Eric?"

"A book." He looked at Charity and said, "It won't take me long. Can, may, I have the next one?"

"How silly of me. Just a moment." She hurried away and returned with the full set in a bag. "Now, you can go straight through without having to visit me."

"I want to visit you."

"You'll always be very welcome. We'll order pizzas."

Eric laughed. "And pop."

"Yes, of course." She settled for a smile, knowing that if she laughed, she'd start crying. She would as soon as she was alone again, but she didn't want an audience.

"Well, thanks again, Charity. It really is appreciated."

"It was a pleasure," she said. "Take care, Eric. Come and see me soon. If you don't, I'll be round to fetch you. No messing."

"I shall," he said. "Thanks for … everything."

She waved as she watched them all leave, and was still waving when they turned at the end of the road. She was pleased that Eric kept waving back. Then she closed her door, relieved and dismal to be on her own again. Back to her study of crimes around the world. Back to her walks in the woods. And back to healthy eating. How she needed to back in her healthy routines.

Tomorrow.

She tapped a familiar number on her telephone, and when there was a reply, she said, "I'd like to order a pizza for six o'clock. Cheese, mushroom and tomato."

And she would toast Eric, with a glass of pop.

THE END